TWIN STUDY

Also by Stacey Richter

My Date With Satan

TWIN STUDY

Stories

STACEY RICHTER

COUNTERPOINT

BERKELEY

HEARTBREAK HOTEL
By Axton/Durden/Presley
©1956 Sony/ATV Songs LLC. All rights administered by Sony/ATV Music Publishing, 8 Music Sq W, Nashville TN 37203. All rights reserved. Used by permission.

HEY NINETEEN
By Donald Fagan/Walter Becker
©1980 Freejunket Music (ASCAP)/Zeon Music (ASCAP)
All rights reserved. Used by permission.

Library of Congress Cataloging-in-Publication Data

Richter, Stacey, 1965–
Twin study : stories / Stacey Richter.
p. cm.
ISBN-13: 978-1-58243-371-4 (alk. paper)
ISBN-10: 1-58243-371-2 (alk. paper)
    I. Title
    PS3568.I35333T85 2007
    813'.54—dc22
    2006035397

2008 Paperback edition: ISBN-13: 978-1-58243-393-6, ISBN-10: 1-58243-393-3

Cover design by Nicole Caputo
Interior design by Timm Bryson
Printed in the United States of America

COUNTERPOINT
2117 Fourth Street
Suite D
Berkeley, CA 94710
www.counterpointpress.com

Distributed by Publishers Group West

10 9 8 7 6 5 4 3 2 1

Contents

TWIN STUDY

I've been a human specimen going on twenty years now, ever since my sister and I were twelve, when my parents enrolled us in the California State University Twin Study. Every four years the two of us, along with several hundred other pairs of identical twins from California, meet in the same depressing chain hotel in Fresno to be tested, prodded, and poked. "You are special!!!" begins the notice for every one of these meetings. Whoopee. I'm special. Not because of anything I've done, no, of course not. I'm special because I'm genetically identical to another person, a person I haven't seen in four years, since the last meeting of the twin study.

Shall I enumerate the many hates associated with this event? First, I hate the hotel. In particular, I can't stand the central atrium; it gives me a bad eighties feeling—of wine bars, terry cloth sweatbands, neon flamingos. It reminds me of that horrible era (between the first and second meeting) when Samantha and I were in our early teens and it was first

1

becoming clear that we were not the same. Of course, we were identical genetically; what's more, we shared a placenta, but inside, in our brains, souls, or hearts, we weren't the same. This became apparent slowly, even though I knew what Samantha was going to say before she said it, and I knew which boys she'd like before she met them, and we always got up at the same time in the night to pee, among other uncanny similarities.

Second, I hate the rooms, with their big, smoked-glass windows overlooking the swimming pool. The glass heats up in the sun and then ticks all night as it cools. I hate the bar, tucked in a dark hole under the escalator, smelling of smoke, though smoking is forbidden in California bars. That's third. Fourth, I hate Fresno, a sad, crumbling town, surrounded on all sides by endless rows of farmland, like an island in a sea of vegetables. I hate the twin researchers, who for the most part are cheerful and kind, dorky in the way of tenured academics—ten years behind in fashion—and do not have dark doubles, I'm sure of it. But most of all, what are we on, six? Yes. I hate seeing Samantha, my twin sister, once every four years.

"Then don't go." This advice comes from Ivan, my husband. "If you dread seeing your sister, don't torture yourself. Stay home."

"That's a good idea," I reply, with conviction, though I've already bought Ivan and me plane tickets and reserved a suite in the horrible hotel. "What about the money?"

"They can shove it," says Ivan. He's older than me by fifteen years, solid and rich from practicing contract law all day long in a high-rise building. Every morning, he shaves his mostly bald head so that it's totally bald. I find him handsome, in a sinister way. Of course it's true that he may not be the most benevolent person in the world. But he's kind to me. And there is much to be said for a man like Ivan, a man who can make me feel very safe even while driving very fast.

"What about science?"

"Fuck science." Ivan sits on the bed and puts on his shoes. A well-dressed man, a successful man, maybe even a little ruthless. I try not to think about that too much but I come across the evidence. A nasty, anonymous letter in the mailbox. A stone through the front window. And then there's his son, Jason, from a previous marriage, who stays over with us one weekend a month. He is, as far as I can tell, a complete monster. But maybe this has nothing to do with Ivan. Thirteen is never a good age.

"I already bought us plane tickets," I confess.

"Okay, if that's what you really want," says Ivan, putting his jacket on, then coming closer and putting his arm around me. "We'll go together." I follow him down the stairs. In the hall he picks up his briefcase, kisses me on the forehead, and sails out the front door. I stand in the doorway in my bathrobe, waving like a fifties housewife. "Call Lana," he yells back, "and let her know the details."

This is the moment I love, right after Ivan leaves for work. I love our big house with the old hardwood floors that gleam like honey in the sunlight. I love the eight-thousand-dollar couch to my right, in the living room, with its thick, down cushions and velvet upholstery. I love the mesquite wood table in the hall, where we pile our mail. I love having it all to myself and knowing that nothing, nothing can ruin our life. Our safe, comfortable, happy life.

Later in the day, I call Lana, Ivan's secretary, and tell her about the trip to Fresno. Lana keeps Ivan's schedule, social and business, and has since before we met.

"He has Jason that weekend," she says.

"Shit."

"So go by yourself."

"I don't want to go by myself," I say. And then, to my surprise, I say, "I want him to meet my sister. Can't Jason switch weekends?"

"Jason cannot switch weekends."

"Are you sure?"

"Honey," Lana lowers her voice, "you should see the divorce agreement. It's like a phone book."

"Oh," I say. I can well imagine. I have, after all, seen my prenuptial. "Then what should we do?"

"Give me your flight number," replies Lana, "I'll get Jason a ticket too."

YOU ARE SPECIAL!!!

Over the twenty-year life span of the California Twin Study, we've gathered vital information that has been of great benefit to the fields of science, social science, and medicine. Some of the data we've collected from our participants has been useful in our understanding of

- Genetics
- Cancer
- Aging and Geriatrics
- Mental Health
- The Changing American Family

We are delighted by your continuing participation in the California Twin Study and look forward to seeing you at our next meeting.

The following weekend will be dizygotic, fraternal twins, the control group. Our weekend is monozygotic, identical twins, the freaks. The hotel lobby is filled with people in their thirties who look either somewhat or exactly alike. Sometimes it's the same face on different bodies—one twin is fatter than the other, or one twin has taken up body building. Often it's the same face with different hair color, hair length, facial hair, hair anything. One twin is an Elvis impersonator—need I say more? Then there are the twins who look exactly alike. It's strange to see them milling around the lobby, talking in pairs or greeting each other with bear hugs. Like most people, I'm not used to seeing identical adults. They all look gigantic. Twinning is something that one encounters in children, or babies, little girls with matching dresses, adorable boys with matching caps; adult twins seem aberrant, even to me. Yet here we are. Some of us even move the same way, or use the same gestures. Our brains are wired up the same. It's a trick of genetics, a dirty trick.

I go to the desk at the far end of the god-awful atrium and pick up my name tag. It says MZ: Amanda 173. That's me, Monozygotic Amanda.

"Has MZ Samantha 173 picked up her tag yet?"

The clerk tells me that she has not. It's perpetually up in the air, of course, whether Samantha will even show up for these weekends. But she always has. She generally needs the money.

Jason and Ivan are on the lobby couches, ignoring each other. "This place sucks," Jason says. Indeed, the hotel remains as noxious as ever, though they've painted the exterior pink since my last visit.

"Maybe you'll like the swimming pool!" I smile brightly.

Jason smiles back. "Gee whiz, Mom, maybe I will!"

"Don't call her Mom," Ivan says.

"Why not? I thought you'd be *happy* if I called her Mom."

"Enough. Just quit it."

Ivan is in a suit. Ivan is always in a suit. Jason is in baggy shorts that seem to be swallowing his beanpole frame. He carries his belongings in a paper bag with the name of a health food store on it. In this sad detail I see a thumbnail sketch of his mother, a harried, distracted, slightly overweight woman Ivan ditched around the time he met me. Jason is also carrying a skateboard and an MP3 player turned up so loudly that I can hear it once the elevator doors close. If I'm not mistaken, there's a woman screaming the words "fuck the pain away" into his ears.

"What's with all the stupid farms here?" Because of the headphones, Jason is yelling.

Ivan stretches the earpiece away from his head. "That's where your food comes from," he tells him. "Where did you think?"

Jason looks like his dad, but softer, moppish, because of his age and the presence of hair—which is greasy and falls into his eyes. I don't know how he manages to be simultaneously sullen and hyper. It must be some trick he does with hormones and Clearasil. In the elevator, I can feel him staring at my breasts. I'm relieved when the doors open and we all tromp down the hall. Lana has managed to exchange our suite for two adjoining rooms. Ivan ushers Jason into his room and shuts the door. Our room sports an intriguing blue theme. Blue bedspread. Blue carpet.

"A romantic weekend in Fresno," says Ivan, pulling me close, "just the three of us."

We've only been married six months so Ivan does a lot of this, pulling me close and so forth. I like it, of course; I love his aftershave. Though at this moment I find myself less appreciative of Ivan and more focused on an idea: I want to show him off to Samantha. Oh God. *See how normal I am? See how nice and rich and stable and normal?*

Without a knock, Jason barrels through the door and jumps onto our bed. He's wearing his swim trunks, and his skinny back is dotted with acne. He rolls onto his back in a kittenish way. "Does your sister look like you?"

"Pretty much. Her hair is usually different." I don't say anything about our breasts, of course. Mine are bigger. I had an operation.

"Hey Dad, don't you think that's weird?"

"No."

"I think it's weird."

Ivan adopts a weary tone. "Okay Jason, why do you think it's weird?"

"Well, you married *her*. Maybe you'll be *attracted* to her sister. Maybe you'll want to grab her ass like you're always grabbing Amanda's."

"Enough!" shouts Ivan. "Get out of here. Go to the pool." Ivan chases him out and slams the door to the adjoining room.

He just wants your attention, I say to myself, but I don't say it to Ivan. I'm not about to intercede on the little monster's behalf.

Ivan takes some work out of his briefcase and settles into a chair. He hasn't come along on this trip just for pleasure—that wouldn't be like Ivan. He has some business to do in Fresno, some deal with some client or some building or some pile of money. Ivan doesn't bother to explain the mechanics of his firm's doings to me. I find this slightly romantic, as though he's working for gangsters. While he takes out his papers, I give the front desk one more call. No, Monozygotic Samantha 173 has not checked in. Not yet.

We used to have better days. That's one thing the twin researchers don't ask us about, though they ask us about

many things—our habits, state of mind, loves, and in-
come—and they take our blood, and measure our brainwaves, and so forth. But they don't ask about watching early
morning cartoons together, laughing at all the same parts, or
running apace through the oaks behind our house, or the
perfectly synchronized water ballet routines we made up as
little girls. They don't ask what it's like to wake up to one's
own double image, realizing you've just had the same dream
about the ocean swallowing the shoreline. They don't ask
about the intimacy, the incredible, terrifying intimacy. Or
what it's like when it's gone.

I feel restless so I go down to mill about with the other
twins in the lobby. Samantha is nowhere in sight. The Elvis
and his non-Elvis twin are sitting on a couch, leafing
through a photo album. My stomach is bothering me so I go
to the bar and try to order a glass of milk.

The bartender is puffy but pretty, an overfed farm girl in
a polyester vest. She answers me with a *what?*

"Milk."

"What?"

"Milk."

We go back and forth about four times before I add, "It
comes from cows." The researchers don't ask about this, either. *Do people understand you when you speak?* The bartender tells me that I'll have to try the coffee shop. Instead,
I wander out of the hotel, into the cavernous entryway—a
ribbon of sidewalk crouching under a huge concrete awning.

And there is Samantha, sitting in an idling car, a boxy number from the sixties. She's smoking a cigarette and chewing gum, her hair streaked blond and clumped, like she's been driving all day. I guess she's been waiting for me. She slides over and opens the passenger door.

"Come on."

I get in and she puts the car in gear. That's all it takes—just stepping off the curb into a car, and it's the two of us again.

"You know what I don't get?"

No hellos, no catching up. It's always like this.

"I don't get why there are no *dog* petting zoos." She rolls down the window and lets her arm hang out. "Then nobody would have to be responsible for one full-time. We could just pay our money and go into a yard full of nice, fluffy golden retrievers and dachshund puppies or whatever."

"Someone would have to clean up all the shit," I say.

"Not me. I paid my money."

I think about it. "That's actually kind of a good idea. There could be a cat section too."

Samantha tosses me a pack of cigarettes. It feels so easy, to just fall into things with Samantha. It feels so easy to just be half of her and let her be half of me. Everything else begins to get dimmer. I half-think of Ivan, back in the room, leafing through papers. I half-think of the twin researchers, sharpening their pencils, waiting to interview us in the morning. *Question: Do people understand you when you speak? Answer: Only my sister.*

"Check this out, up here on the left," she says. "Hair sperm."

There's a strip mall with a haircutting place called "Hair & Perm" beside the road; the ampersand has been placed unfortunately close to the word "Perm."

"That's really funny."

"You always say, 'That's really funny,' instead of laughing."

"I know, because you always complain about it."

I lean against the car door and look Samantha over. She's blonder than me, which is new, certainly grubbier, wearing jeans and a tank top versus my tasteful linen suit. As always, she has our long legs and thick hair and golden skin that tans out to a flat brown. We are nice-looking girls—it's hard to mess that up. Though some years it seems as if Samantha is trying her best. I check her hands. They look good, smooth, with clipped nails. Not like last time, when her fingers were covered with cigarette burns and her eyes were so bloodshot I thought she'd been punched.

"Do you think, since there's no aesthetic plan in the suburbs, like there was in Haussmann's Paris or Vienna or wherever, that this planlessness is Zen?" Samantha chucks her gum out the window. "Do you think the suburbs, with their lack of human design, are an expression of God's plan?"

"Well, a lot of suburbs are planned. There are master planned communities, like Brasilia and all those retirement towns in the Sun Belt."

"I would like to be a slave in a master planned community."

"That might be good for you."

"I could break out my leather underwear."

Samantha has piloted us out of the dying downtown and into the thriving sprawl. The suburbs here look the same as the suburbs anywhere in the country—the same stores, the same chain restaurants serving the same chain food. We're not the only clones.

"You know what I really wish?" There's a tremor to Samantha's voice. "I wish I lived in a world where nobody knew how they felt about anything."

"Really? That's weird. I'm not sure what a world without feeling would be like."

"It wouldn't be a world without feeling," Samantha explains, "it would be a world where no one *knew* how they felt. No reflection. No self-reflection."

"No unhappy feelings."

"No guilt," says Samantha. "People would just do things and then feel really satisfied with themselves."

I think of Ivan, his brow serene after a day of cutthroat litigation. "You know how you just meet some people, and after five minutes you can tell they've never felt guilty their whole lives?"

"Boys!" she says.

"Yeah, for one, boys. Grown men. They're happy being jerks."

"And then we're all, 'I'm sorry, I'm sorry! I'm sorry everything isn't perfect. I'm sorry I'm not Shirley fucking Temple making everyone happy with my little face.'" Samantha is excited now, steering with one hand and smoking with the other.

"It's pathetic."

"I wish I had a cock. I read an article that said PMS killed Sylvia Plath."

"You've got to admit, Sylvia Plath killed Sylvia Plath."

"Oh no. I don't got to admit anything." Samantha grins at me, a too-big grin. Something is going on. We are in for a Samantha moment. Samantha loves dramas, big, small, whatever. When we were kids, Samantha would always beg me to go first, but when it came time, she'd throw an arm across me and bolt forward, itching to do something daring or stupid. Now she stops in the middle of a suburban neighborhood, in front of a row of identical houses, tiled roofs, typical Taco Bell–style architecture. I notice that Samantha has a piece of paper in her hand. It says:

FOUND:
PUG

And then there's an address.
"Are you coming with me?"
"I guess."
Samantha leads the way to the front door of the house. She rings the bell and a middle-aged woman answers wearing the modern-day version of the apron: a sweat suit. Samantha smiles and begins to speak. Even to me, she sounds sincere. This has always been her great talent—convincing people. She can talk her way into and then back out of any situation. I think it's what enables her to live without any fixed address or steady job, though I'm not really sure how Samantha lives these days.
"We lost him about four days ago," Samantha says, facing the woman squarely, looking her in the eye. "We had guests and they left the gate open."

"We found the dog *five* days ago," the woman says. She has a plain Midwestern face, no makeup, a practical face without time for foolishness.

"Monday?"

"Yes."

"That's when we lost him."

The woman seems suspicious of Samantha, but then she uncrosses her arms and half-smiles—she wants to believe. "We thought it was a female."

"Yes," Samantha is loose, seamless when she lies, "I know, it's confusing. When we got her my sister kept saying she looked like a him, so finally we just named her Him." Samantha laughs. "Everyone gets mixed up."

What can the woman say to this? It's so ridiculous, I expect her to slam the door in our faces. But Samantha has something I don't have, something the researchers can't quantify: charisma. I find it maddening.

The woman goes inside and comes back with a pug dog wheezing on the end of a red leash.

"Him!" exclaims Samantha. The dog trots over and licks her hand.

She thanks the woman and turns to usher the pug down the walk. It waddles to the car and hops in the front seat like an old hand. I have to shove it over to sit down. The dog looks around placidly, its froggy eyes bulging, its skin hanging around its compact body. It starts to pant.

"Check it out," she says. "These things cost about a thousand dollars new."

"Is that really your dog?"

Samantha looks at me and says, "That's really funny."

"No, really."

"It's your dog," she says. "I got it for you."

"I don't want it."

"Why not?"

"I just don't."

"Okay, fine. I guess it's my dog." Then she puts her face in her hands and begins to sob.

I've been trying figure out what's wrong with Samantha for years. What is she? Bipolar or borderline or schizophrenic or manic or what? Whatever it is, my chance of having it as well is around 80 percent. But she doesn't seem to have any of these conditions, not really, not typically, according to the researchers. Well, according to one particular researcher, Kevin, a bearded psychology professor I charmed one night at the hotel bar, a couple of meetings ago. It's amazing what an amicable one-night stand can accomplish. He's been my man on the inside ever since, a steady source of information. About me, of course, but mostly about Samantha.

"Samantha is just volatile," Kevin explained, at the last meeting. I wasn't married yet but he was; he had made it clear that our *love affair* was over. "It's not necessarily an illness."

"But how can she be so volatile when I'm not?"

"Well," he stroked his beard, "the thing we've learned is that monozygotic twins raised apart—in different environments—still have about fifty percent of their personality traits in common."

"Fine." I'm always impatient with Kevin's professorial tone—just because he's the researcher and I'm the subject doesn't mean he's a genius and I'm a dolt. "Then twins raised in the same environment must have even more."

"That's the fascinating thing. Twins raised together also have about fifty percent of their personality traits in common." He raised his eyebrows—a significant look.

"Okay, professor. Meaning what?"

"Well, most identical twins don't like to hear this, but we attribute the fifty percent variation to the fact that they *were* raised together."

"Oh, I see. That fifty percent is us *trying* to be different from one another."

"Exactly. Trying, on some level."

"We stake our spot. I'm the good twin. Samantha's the evil twin."

"I wouldn't call Samantha evil, personally. She's prone to substance abuse. You may be too. She's more creative."

I cringed. I'd been hearing about her creativity my whole life. "So I'm the boring one, and she's the scarf-dancer."

"Basically."

I thought about this while Kevin chewed handfuls of bar peanuts and gazed around the room. He was short, with narrow hands and a baby face. The beard was a nice try but he still looked like a graduate student. The bartender had carded him.

"What if we had been one person? With the same genetics, but just one of us, without the other to react to. What would that person be like?"

"That's what happens to everyone else," Kevin said. "But you're a twin."

"Right," I said. "I'm special."

———————

Samantha and I drive back downtown in silence, though she keeps crying for a while. She turns the car around under the concrete awning and then sits behind the wheel, eyes red, staring at the instrument panel.

"Are you coming in?"

"Maybe later." She rubs the pug's head. It's wheezing through its little stoved-in nose. I wonder if she'll ever get over this. I wonder if she's ever gotten over anything in her whole life.

"It's just not a good time for a pet right now."

"No, that's fine." Samantha waves her hand.

"Call me in my room. I want you to meet my husband."

"You got *married?*"

"Yes, of course. I would have invited you if I had known how to reach you."

"You got *married?* My God. Why?"

"Love," I say, but it doesn't sound quite right.

Samantha starts tapping the pug on the nose. Something about her seems about ten years old. This makes me want to throttle her. "Do you want to know why I'm naming her Diego?" she asks.

"Okay."

"Because she's bug-eyed and fat and a communist, like Diego Rivera."

"How do you know she's a communist?"

"The red leash. And she was free."

That night I lie in bed with Ivan's arms around me, listening to the windows ticking. I don't know what happened to Samantha. She never called.

If you feel a statement is **true** or **mostly true**, fill in the circle marked **T**. If a statement is **false** or **usually not true**, fill in the circle marked **F**. If a statement does not apply to you or pertains to something you don't know about, make no mark on the answer sheet, but please try to give a response to every statement.

1. I would enjoy beating a cardsharp at his own game.
2. There are times when I am certain that people in high places are monitoring my thoughts.
3. If I were a journalist, I would very much enjoy working the theater beat.
4. Willful horses should be paddled or whipped.
5. I never have strong-smelling bowel movements.
6. If I could take something from a store and be sure I was not seen, I would probably do it.

7.   The top of my scalp is sore to the
       touch.

Every year, they give us the same ridiculous, ancient psychological test, the Michigan Comprehensive Personality Evaluation, and every year, I try to pick answers *I know* Samantha will not pick. After all, we're only supposed to have 50 percent of our personality traits in common. And yet, every year, according to Kevin, Samantha and I pick the same answers to virtually every question.

I'm struggling with number 3: *If I were a journalist, I would very much enjoy working the theater beat.* For me, the answer is F, I hate the theater. It's too slow. Samantha, though, always liked plays and even worked on one or two during high school, when she wasn't busy smoking pot with her stoner friends. But there's something about this question—the way it feels like a pale attempt to sniff out homosexual tendencies—that makes me think that Samantha would mark F in an attempt to be subversive, even though her true answer is probably T. Yes, that's it. I decide that Samantha will answer F; therefore I will answer T.

My hand hovers above the bubble marked T. But wait! Since we always choose the same answer, I realize that this time I should invert my reasoning process now, at the last minute, and flop over to F.

F is the answer.

I answer each question via this rather laborious process, with the last-minute flop.

Later, I come across Kevin in one of the long, carpeted hallways of the hotel.

"Ninety-seven percent!" he says, holding his hand up for a high-five. "Same as last time!"

"Damn it."

Kevin grabs my hand and veers into me. He keeps coming until he's backed me into a windowless room with a table and a soda machine. Kevin looks at me. I look at Kevin. His narrow fingers are gripping my hand like tentacles.

"You two certainly are interesting."

I've become used to a kind of abstracted fondness from Kevin, so I'm surprised by his intense demeanor—magnified by a spray of wild eyebrow hairs I've never noticed before. I wonder if they've sprouted due to advancing age—or did he give up trimming them? I ponder this while Kevin clutches me.

He leans closer. "I could tell you things about your sister."

"Go ahead."

"I can't."

"Why not?"

"I signed a confidentiality agreement."

I laugh. "That never stopped you before."

"Yeah, well," he crosses his arms across his chest, "that was then. Things are different now."

"Why are you acting like this?"

"Like what?"

"Like you want to fuck me."

The blood rushes to Kevin's cheeks. "I never said that."

"You didn't *say* it."

"It's not that," he mops his sleeve over his face. "It's just this thing with my wife." He lets out a long sigh. "Our relationship is kind of rocky right now."

"I'm sorry to hear that."

"It's just this thing." Kevin stares at the floor. "I love her. I do. It's just that she won't perform certain sexual acts . . . "

"Okay, stop."

"I really want to get this off my chest."

"I don't want to hear it."

"Amanda," Kevin extends a hand toward me—five tentacles, imploring and threatening.

"What?" I'm already halfway around the table and heading for the door.

He has dark circles under his eyes. "You're so pretty," he says, in a rancorous tone.

I slide past him, into the hall.

———

A little later, during the break for lunch, I find Ivan lying by the pool. He looks relaxed and tan, splayed out with a *Business Week* by his side. He has lots of hair on his chest—the emblem of the alpha male. Though quite a few people are using the pool, all the nearby chaises are empty. I attribute this to Ivan's formidable air; he carries it with him like a force field. But there are moments when it evaporates. Like when he plays the piano.

"Where's Jason?" he says.

"I have no idea."

"I thought you took him shopping."

"I didn't take him shopping. Why do you think I took Jason shopping?"

"Because you said so," Ivan replies.

"When?"

"A little while ago."

"I didn't say that."

"Yes you did."

Oh no. I think I see what is going on here. But Ivan would never fall for it. Besides, Samantha hasn't tried this for a long time, not since my high school boyfriend, the football player, bought himself a red convertible.

"That wasn't me. That was my sister."

"Oh," Ivan says, mildly, as though I'd just pointed out an interesting item floating in the pool.

"Don't you know me?"

"Of course I know you."

I feel so angry—at that moment—I don't think I've ever been so angry at Ivan. "She doesn't even look like me. Her hair is streaked, she smokes, she's thinner, she acts all . . . whacked out. Ivan! Look at me."

He looks at me, calm and patient, the man I married. Solid. The man who flies off the handle at everyone except me.

"This is me. I'm not her. Look at me. My breasts are bigger."

"Your breasts?"

"Ask Jason. He knows."

"Amanda, what do you expect? If you girls are up to tricks like that—identical twins," he squints at me through the sun. "Any jury would find me innocent."

"*I'm* not up to anything."

"You said you'd take him shopping." He closes his eyes and settles his bald, bronzing head on a rolled up towel. "Somebody took him away, thank God."

"It wasn't me."

"I know."

"She's not me."

"Of course she's not."

Of course. Why should I expect Ivan to be any different? Everyone thinks we're the same. *We* even think we're the same. That's why we can only stand to see each other once every four years. Who wants to see their identity swallowed up by their double? I certainly feel poorer for it. The only people who seem to profit are the researchers. They get to learn if both of us stutter or get cancer of the pancreas; they get to learn if both of us marry swarthy plumbers or enjoy table tennis. They seem so sure that twins hold clues to the mystery of identity: what depends on threads of DNA winding and unwinding in our cells, and what do we glean from the world? Kevin and his friends are trying to study what makes us *us*—but not us per se, not the twins. We're the freaks. They want to know what we mean for normal people. Why do normals divorce, sicken, hate licorice, refuse to perform certain sexual acts?

Is it genetics or environment? As if the data could ever tell us why we feel the way we feel.

I order a drink and settle into a chaise. After a while, Samantha shows up. She's riding Jason's skateboard with the pug laboring at her side. Poor Diego. I don't know what she was bred for, but it wasn't running. Jason is trotting along behind them. Under his curtain of bangs, his face looks different.

"Check out my shirt!" He points at his chest, where the words DESIGNATED DRIVER stretch across in big, iron-on letters. I grasp what it is about his face: he's smiling.

Samantha jumps off the skateboard and plops down beside me. "The thrift stores around here are unbelievable. We found the greatest stuff." She reaches into a plastic bag and pulls out a green bowling shirt. On the back it says: SEVENTH-DAY ADVENTIST DENTISTS.

"That's really funny."

"Want it? It's one of a kind."

"Yes." I'm surprised by myself, because usually Samantha is the one who wears the thrift-store shirts. But I can't pass this one up. "I hear you met my husband."

"Uh-huh."

"He thought you were me."

"He did?" Samantha looks surprised.

"Did you tell him that?"

She looks as if she's tasted something sour: this is our lying face. "I don't think so."

"It's a yes-or-no question."

Samantha is leaning back next to me on the chaise, curling and uncurling Diego's tail. Jason has pulled up a chair beside her. He gazes at her with adoration. He says, "Hey Dad!"

Ivan, sunbathing and half-asleep, grunts.

"Samantha took me to this restaurant where we ate balls of raw meat!"

"It's Armenian," she explains.

"We fed some to Diego."

"She liked it." Samantha is wearing just a bikini top and jeans. She's as brown as maple syrup and has muscles all up and down her arms and back. I guess she's been going to the gym.

"You shouldn't eat raw meat." Ivan's eyes are still closed. "You'll get cholera."

"Samantha did it."

He looks up. "That's bright. If she jumped off a cliff, would you follow?"

Jason cocks his head. "Maybe."

"Beautiful. I'm going in the water." Ivan ambles off and wades into the pool, holding his magazine above his waist.

As soon as he's gone, Samantha turns to me, her hands folded in her lap. "Your husband is intimidating. His after-shave smells expensive."

"That's because it *is* expensive," I snap. Diego is leaning against my leg. I bend down to pet her. Something is bothering me. Something is bothering me a lot.

"Samantha, why can't you be my stepmom?" Jason says, right on cue.

"She's your step-aunt," I tell him. "You can call her Auntie Sam."

"Don't call me Sam," she says. "She's saying that because I hate it."

"You should wear sunscreen," I tell Samantha, "you're too tan."

I can feel us falling into a rhythm—it's like loneliness and the antithesis of loneliness at the same time. And it really is like falling, exciting or terrifying, depending on what's below. I say, "Kevin has a hate-crush on me."

"Who's Kevin?"

"The one with the Lenin beard." I pick up Diego and put her in my lap. She starts licking my hand.

"Right, I know him. He has the funny eyebrows. Did you engender the hate, or is it women in general?"

"What's a hate-crush?" Jason asks.

I ignore him. "I think his wife engendered the hate. But now it's directed at women in general."

"What are you guys talking about?" Jason looks at us sideways. "Is this your secret twin language?"

"No!" we both say, in unison.

Samantha turns to Jason. "A hate-crush is when a man likes a woman a lot, so he's mean to her."

For some reason, this makes Jason blush. "I thought that was over in third grade."

"No," Samantha says. "Sadly, no. Promise me you won't do it. It's extremely uncool."

"Okay," Jason says.

"Be nice to the girls you like. Even if it's a little scary."

He's nodding, really soaking it in. It occurs to me that Samantha may be changing the course of his life.

"I don't have anywhere to pin this." She holds up the name tag that says "MZ Samantha 173" and tries to pin it to her bikini strap.

"That's what you get for not wearing a shirt."

"Wait," Samantha smiles, "check this out." She takes the pin and pushes it through the tough skin of her outer elbow. She fastens the clasp. It stays there as she flexes her arm.

"Wow," says Jason.

"That's disgusting," I say.

"Come on," she says to Jason, putting on her sunglasses, "I have an appointment on the inside."

They gather their things and go into the hotel. It takes me a while to realize she's left Diego with me. I guess Samantha never has been very good at taking care of things.

———

No one has asked for my opinion of the California Twin Study, but if I were to be asked, I would tell the researchers to stop doing all the things that make us feel like rats. The lines of colored tape in the hallways that usher us from room to room are especially inane, and after certain tests, we are offered donuts—why not lumps of cheese? Then there is the underlying philosophy to all this testing, that any information we may be given is too much information. So, I go into a room, I lie on a padded table, and a woman in a white coat tapes ice-cold electrodes to my head. When I ask her what they're for, she says, "Taking measurements." When I ask what kind of measurements, she says, "Important ones." Then she leaves me in the half-darkened room, with instructions to relax. But I know what they're doing: measuring my brainwaves to see if they match Samantha's.

For a while I try to think my own, idiosyncratic thoughts; then that seems too Samantha-like so I go for some dull, average thoughts; then I realize this is the same road I went down with the personality test. I don't have any of this figured out anyway. I don't know how much of me is a part of her no matter what. We grew up together. We're the same genetically. Maybe the desire to be singular is just another thing we share and somewhere, in some other room, Samantha is lying with wires attached to her head, trying to think thoughts that I wouldn't think. Finally, I give up trying to be original and fall asleep on the table. Almost immediately I begin to have the dream: the ocean swells, enormous waves sparkle in the sun and rise above the beach. Then, the entire shoreline is swallowed up—houses, cars, cliffs, umbrellas—they're all washed away, and all that's left is a great expanse of blue water: nothing. Everything.

A few hours later, I find Samantha sitting on the carpet in one of the long hallways, slumped over a line of yellow tape. She's crying.

I sigh. "What's wrong now?"

"You're *married*." She wipes the snot off her face. It's a nice face, somehow prettier on Samantha (I even got Kevin to admit this), more transparent and broad. It's a little icier on me, with a knot between the eyebrows I keep meaning to get Botoxed.

"So what?"

"You're just . . . normaler."

"You say that like it's a good thing."

"It *is* good. You're the good one, remember?"

I laugh. "Okay, let's get this out in the open once and for all. True or false: The top of my scalp is sore to the touch."

"True!" Samantha touches her part. "Right here. It drives me crazy!"

I touch my own head and am surprised to find I have a sore spot there too. I try another. "True or false: I would enjoy beating a cardsharp at his own game."

"True! Wouldn't you?"

"Yes. Do you always answer them truthfully?"

"Of course." Samantha sniffs. "How about you?"

"I try to pick whatever one I think you wouldn't."

She laughs at this. "Then you must switch it."

"Yes." I feel dispirited. Of course Samantha knows all about me and my ways.

"You always did love to lie," she says.

"You left the dog with me."

"I did?"

"I'm not keeping it."

"I know."

I look at her, her face red from crying. I can't remember the last time I cried. Even Ivan, when we got married, became a little teary. But not me. I'm the stable one.

Later that day, Kevin locates me and apologizes. His eyebrows are smoother and he looks embarrassed. Too much work, he explains, shoving his hands into his pockets. Way too much coffee. Then, as a peace offering, he tells me what it is he's learned about Samantha: she's pregnant. He doesn't know if she knows. And, in the grand tradition of the California Twin Study, no one has mentioned this to her.

I think about this through dinner and after, in our rooms, where Jason refuses to settle down. Ivan tells him he can call for room service, he can order Nintendo with the remote, but he keeps jumping on his bed like a little boy while Ivan repeats "Jason," in a threatening tone.

"So what do you think about Samantha?" I lean up against the doorjamb between our rooms. "She's kind of a loose cannon, isn't she?"

"She's okay," Ivan says. "Jason!" Jason jumps higher. Hanks of greasy hair stream upward from his head. Ivan looks at his watch. "She's not as unpleasant as you described."

"I," Jason jumps once on each word, "like, her, more, than," his face is turning red, "either, of, you."

"For God's sake, stop that," Ivan says.

"You should have seen her before. She's reformed or something. She used to be even more, I don't know, disturbed. She took drugs."

"She didn't seem that disturbed to me," says Ivan.

Jason is now making a "va" sound with each jump, like a car that won't turn over.

"You can tell she's nothing like me though, can't you?"

Ivan laughs. "Well, there are similarities."

"I can tell," Jason chants.

"Excuse me, I was asking your dad."

"Boy, can I."

"Okay, Jason. I'm asking your dad."

"Jason, stop that right now," Ivan roars.

"He isn't going to stop."

"Jason!"

"He isn't going to stop until you quit telling him to."

"Jason! I said now!"

I go back to our room and turn on the TV. Finally, Ivan just shuts the door to the adjoining room and bolts it. I can hear the *squeak squeak* of Jason jumping on the bed for a while, even as Ivan eases me down on our own bed and starts pulling off my blouse. He lies beside me and unclasps my bra. Jason has quieted down but then he starts knocking at the door. Lightly, at first, but then he's pounding and crying "Dad," in a scared voice. I guess thirteen isn't really that old. Two or three years ago, he would have been too young to leave without a babysitter. I guess I should feel sorry for him. But mostly I feel annoyed.

"Jesus," says Ivan.

He excuses himself and slips into Jason's room. I brace myself for another round of screaming but don't hear anything for a long time. Then I hear Ivan's voice, very faintly, coming through the door. He's not yelling. He's singing.

Here's what I know: life is ordinary. Dreams, sickness, joy, grieving, loving our children—everybody experiences these things. Everyone is full of goodness and dark longings. We all have the capacity for sacrifice, for betrayal, for wildness. All of us have woken up one morning and said to ourselves: *I want everything, everything, now, now,* but we grow up. It goes away; the longing to take the whole world inside ourselves, to make every second count, to live many lives. We spend our days lost in activity. We marry rich men who can never fully know us, and we like the idea. Or—what? We end up like Samantha—with our feelings smacking us like waves, over and over, half-drowning us, never getting a chance to learn to swim, never even being smart enough to get out of the water. I *know.* That could have been me.

I ask Kevin if it could be me again.

"I'm not sure what you mean," he says. He's sitting surrounded by papers, questionnaires, file boxes—he'll spend the rest of the year working on this weekend's data.

"I mean, could I be like Samantha? Could I be volatile? Could I run around claiming dogs that aren't mine and crying at everything, could I charm thirteen-year-old boys, could I eat raw meat—that kind of thing."

"Well," Kevin says, "you *are* like Samantha. If anyone could, it would be you. But . . . "

"But what?"

"You aren't her."

"Not right now. But I have been."

Sunday evening, after we're finished with the last of the tests, Samantha and Diego and I take another ride in her Impala. We drive out into the farmland, through rows of vegetables fanning out along the road, lettuce and peas and tomatoes and cotton, squash and soybeans, all growing fat in the California sun. The plants look beautiful but they're all sprayed down with toxic chemicals. The migrant workers get sick from working with them, or so I've read.

I ask her to pull over beside a field of cherry tomatoes. They're hanging off the stalks like green pearls and the air is spiked with their pumpkin smell. All that produce, all that ripening—it's an incredible abundance, and it fills me with greed.

We sit there in silence as the engine cools down.

"Ivan's not that nice, is he?" Samantha gazes out the windshield at the tomatoes. "Jason says he's an asshole."

"Jason's thirteen."

"Yeah, but he's not an idiot."

I consider this. "Ivan's not that bad. He can be an asshole, obviously. He doesn't take any shit. He's rich and successful and feels he deserves all that he has and more."

"What's that like?"

"It's steady. It's very calming."

"Yeah. It sounds easy. It sounds kind of great."

Diego's head is in my lap. She's snoring. Already, I know, Samantha and I are thinking the same thing.

"Does he always wear that aftershave?"

"Every day."

"I like it."

"So do I."

I smile and pull my dress off over my head. Samantha watches me with almost no expression—just a little disbelief around the corners of her eyes. Because usually she's the one, with her Samantha moments, who changes everything. But not this time. I take off my bra and camisole and hand them to her.

Samantha starts to smile. Then she takes off her bikini top and ripped jeans. She hands me her cigarettes. She smoothes down her hair and puts on my linen sundress, my beige sandals. Now we're both giggling. We used to do this all the time, back when we had the same dreams. Sometimes we'd do it for just a few hours, but other times we kept it up for days, months even. I would be Samantha, and she would be Amanda. I would be creative and spontaneous, and she would be methodical and calm. I'd carry her books and take her tests and use her toothbrush and sleep in her bed. No one knew. Even our parents were utterly fooled. We thought they deserved it for dressing us alike, cutting our hair the same, taking us to the same piano teacher who taught us the same pieces to play at the same recitals. There have been times when I've even wondered, over the years, if we ever switched once and forgot to switch back.

Maybe I've been the volatile one all along.

"What do I need to know?" Samantha asks.

I have it all laid out: I open my ostrich purse. "Here are my credit cards," I say. "This is the code to our alarm, these are the keys to the house, here's my driver's license. This is my address book, with our friends' names highlighted, and my calendar with birthdays and anniversaries indicated. This is where I take yoga," I hand her a flyer, "usually on Tuesdays and Thursdays. This is my smoothie punch card. I like the femme boost."

"What else?"

"Kevin told me you're pregnant."

Samantha laughs. I have no idea what this means. For once, I have the giddy sensation of having absolutely no idea what my sister is thinking. And I don't want to know. But she does say, "You don't have to do this for me."

"I'm not."

We switch places and I drive my sister back to the hotel. She leans back in the passenger seat, an arm hanging out the window into the warm California sky. I'm surprised to see how good she looks in my dress. Conventionalism suits her remarkably well. She looks calmer, more focused, now that she's inhabiting my skin. You don't miss the breasts, either. No one will ever know. Except Jason, of course.

I stop the car in front of the lobby. Samantha bends over and kisses Diego so that I'm staring at the tender spot on the top of her head.

"Goodbye, Amanda," I say.

"Goodbye, Samantha," she replies, and then without a glance back she slams the door and walks off, wobbling slightly on her heels, until she's swallowed up by the smoked-glass doors of the hotel.

I put the car in gear and turn it around, Diego at my side, and drive off crying into the sea of vegetables.

VELVET

Velvet came into the family in the usual way, through a classified ad in the local newspaper: CUTE PUPPIES FREE TO GOOD HOME! The mistress of the house and her twelve-year-old daughter drove to an address in Sunny-slope, where they ventured into a stucco townhouse and picked her out of a cardboard box. She was an Australian terrier mix, rat-sized, though later she grew to be as large as a raccoon. The girl named her Velvet, possibly in a tribute to her silky undercoat (which disappeared within three months), possibly because she simply liked the name. The little girl swore to feed her and house-train her and dress her in tiny plaid coats when it rained, but after several weeks spent holding the puppy so constantly that the dog was damp with hand-sweat, her infatuation faded and the care of Velvet reverted to the mistress of the house. The mistress did not particularly want a puppy and was preoccupied with other tasks; as a result, Velvet grew up to be an unruly, unchecked, sneaky kind of dog, barely compliant enough to avoid getting her ass smacked by a rolled-up newspaper. She peed outside (most of the time), she came when she was called (if there was food involved), she chewed on shoes and electrical cords and devoured used Kleenex. She was a jumper and a barker and an underbed sulker; once, she managed to steal a frozen chicken from a grocery bag and drag it behind the couch. Mostly, though, she liked to hurl herself at doors, expressing her ardent desire to run freely through the neighborhood, fuck leashes.

Yet there was no denying the cuteness that was Velvet. She possessed the stubborn happiness that is the mark of the terrier breed, with alert, dark eyes and a pink tongue, which dangled from her mouth like a scrap of ribbon. She seldom used her stubby legs for walking, preferring to trot from place to place, holding her square head high and puffing out her chest beneath her coat, which was brown and black and stiff as an old rag. Her dark eyes were always scanning for opportunity. It was clear to any observer that Velvet existed in a world loosely bounded by the temporal zone of the now. She was in the moment but straining against it, into the near future, where, if she was a lucky girl, the door might slip open and she'd wriggle her way to freedom. When the members of the family entered and exited the house, they cracked the door half a foot and wedged themselves through the gap to prevent her escape. They regarded her jolly face with wariness. It was hard to really love something that always wanted to flee—who clearly preferred to be elsewhere. But Velvet didn't notice; she felt loved, she felt like a princess. Every evening, she gazed at the family from her position of squat royalty, waiting for them to drop the scraps of food on the floor that were her tribute.

But the family was easily distracted from its duties as dog-tenders; situations involving children and visitors in particular led to lapses that allowed her to escape. Once Velvet was outside, she'd go running through the streets of the neighborhood, running, running, running on her stubby legs. Velvet loved the loft she got when she leapt off the curb into the street—legs extended, ears flattened, fur fluffed. She felt that her destiny was nearby, she was almost there, and she would run to it. It was true that she wasn't sure exactly what this was, though possibly it involved a field full of other terriers and rubber balls and declawed cats, as well as chances to hump and be humped (though she'd been spayed), and the opportunity to smell beneath the tails of many, many dogs, but mainly other terriers, dogs who were like Velvet but slightly inferior, with thinner coats and less piercing barks, who would be willing to be chased, or else to vomit up their food and let Velvet eat it.

Around the time the girl entered high school, the family moved to a bigger house in a swanky subdivision on the edge of the open desert. The mistress had been dreaming of this house her whole life, a lovely house where she'd picked out the furniture and the drapes as well as yards and yards of thick, white carpet. In honor of the carpet, Velvet was to become an outside dog. There was a large, fenced yard—the fence was wooden, with chain link on one side—and a dog house and a lawn and a spigot that dripped cool water into

Velvet's bowl. The girl could go outside to play with Velvet whenever she wanted, but there wasn't really any playing with her. All the girl could do was stand there while the dog hurled herself against the girl's knee socks. Sometimes she'd throw a ball and Velvet would seize it in her jaws and freeze. When the girl approached, she'd dash away with a tail wag that taunted: *tag, you're it.*

Not surprisingly, Velvet was left alone in the yard most of the time, chasing birds and digging holes (bad dog). So it came to be that Velvet wasn't really anyone's pet—as the family dog, she was loved in the abstract but she was not in any sense actively loved. Velvet would stand outside on the patio and whine and throw herself against the sliding glass door while the family ate dinner on the other side; when she grew tired of that she would press herself forward and lick the door—avidly, meticulously, from right to left and back again until a plaque of dried spit formed on the glass. Now, instead of squeezing through the door to prevent Velvet from squirming out, the family had to do the opposite and squeeze through the door to keep Velvet from wriggling back in.

What Velvet finally did to kill time was take up barking in earnest. She liked to bark in rounds of four: *I—Am—A—Dog! I—Am—A—Dog!* She flung herself into barking with all the energy of her previous, indoor life, but she'd begun to devote a larger portion of the day to sleeping. Her world had transformed, and her gusto with it. Gone was the carpet, the floor scraps, the dark beneath the bed; now there was grass, ant flesh, and a sky full of lightning. At night, she saw strange things moving on the other side of the chain link—lizards, rabbits, and something even more mind-blowing: wild dogs with a wild scent who ran in groups of three or four and yipped and howled with an eerie sound. When they wandered into view, the hair on Velvet's back bristled. She rushed the fence, declaring her selfhood: *I— Am—A—Dog!* The coyotes sniffed the fence one time, gave her a disdainful glance, and loped off.

It became her nightly habit, after the family was asleep, to stand on the clipped grass, her pink bows trembling (she'd been to the groomer), listening to the coyotes howl. Once, there was a crashing sound as they tipped over the family's garbage can. Velvet paced the lawn. Could she be one of them? A wild thing? A wild, unruly, carrion-eating, humping and yowling beast? After all, She Was A Dog. But they howled and mated and hunted and yipped and the answer was: Not likely, little poochie.

One day a meter reader left the side gate ajar and Velvet strolled out of her little yard into the open air. It was afternoon and the shadows of cacti and rocks were already lengthening against the ground. When she raised her nose and sniffed, she detected nothing more exotic than orange blossoms, but the air was vibrating with small, silver squiggles and she could feel surges of life pulsing through the earth and into her paws. She realized that there was no chain on her collar, no one near to grab her. It occurred to her what she was *free, free, fucking free!* Velvet lit out down the street, her walnut-sized heart pumping, galloping with all her strength toward something—something!—and though the nature of the something was unclear, she knew that it lay not behind her but ahead. After running for a while she found several items worthy of consideration: a pile of loose dirt, suitable for digging; a fence enclosing an old, matted poodle; and a rock with a lizard under it. But these things were not satisfying, so Velvet trotted on, urged by a yearning that pulled her into the desert as firmly as would any leash.

By the time the sun began to dip below the horizon, she found herself standing in the open on top of an intoxicating rise. The earth beneath her was looped with trails of urine and the smell of rotted flesh. She lowered her head to sniff, then rolled in the stinkiest spot. It was the coyotes, she was sure of it. When Velvet inhaled, she had the sensation of being surrounded by secrets she could feel but not understand, a primal knowledge that extended beyond her yard and the cubes of cheese lobbed into her mouth and the girl who stroked her ears—way beyond.

Something rustled in the bushes, and of course she smelled them before she saw them: three lean coyotes with long, bushy tails sloping toward the ground. They had lolling tongues and black-edged ears. They impressed Velvet immediately—they were doglike but they weren't dogs; they were even more fascinating, slinky and bad, like big kids in leather jackets, smoking. Velvet began to pant. Then she barked: *I—Am—A—Dog!* while they stared at her, visibly disgusted. The biggest walked up to her and lunged for her throat. Velvet sprang to the side, pouncing into play position with her butt in the air and her tail wagging madly. Another moved toward her flank with bared teeth and Velvet feinted left. The front-runner lunged at her collar.

Of course Velvet didn't understand that they wanted to eat her. She didn't know that small dogs and stray cats formed a good part of the suburban coyote diet, along with cottontails and bugs and road kill and garbage; besides, they weren't that much bigger than she was and Velvet had always regarded herself as rather mighty. But the coyotes were practiced killers and Velvet was out of her depth—so far, in fact, that it didn't occur to her to behave like prey. Instead she wagged her tail and yapped with glee. She dodged sideways; she ran a few feet and waited for them to chase her. *You're it*, she barked, *You're it, it, it!*

She was a foolish dog, a lucky dog too, because after chasing her for a while the coyotes began to get annoyed. Her squatness made her agile, though she wasn't very fast, and it became evident (as they pursued her around a nasty stand of cholla) that she wasn't the dumb, ready-to-eat morsel they'd taken her for. She was more of a rodeo clown: ridiculous, exasperating, and doused with the weird, cereal odor of dog food. After a while they lost interest and wandered into the brush in search of easier pickings—things that were already dead, for example, or hairless baby bunnies with their eyes still closed.

Velvet watched them slink into the bushes, then perked up her ears and jogged after them. She perceived all manner of flight as an invitation and this one was especially welcome. At last she was being summoned into a world she'd dreamed about so often (stuck in the yard with a spit-softened chew toy)—a world that smelled like two things she basically never got to experience: fucking and death. Fucking! And death! She could imagine it, a vista of dead things and humping, she saw it even as the coyotes drew farther away, outpacing her easily with their smooth, intradesert lope. They headed toward a dark gap below the road and disappeared into the ground.

Velvet ran to the spot and stopped. It was a hole in the side of a hill, a galvanized drainage ditch that tunneled under the road, two feet high with a layer of sand at the bottom. It smelled like rotted wood and motor oil. There were no yellowed newspapers nearby, no empty cans or people-trace. When she cocked her ears, she could hear the coyotes' paws and the soft, birdlike yipping they made to each other as they disappeared out the far end. Velvet licked her nose. She wanted to be one of them. She wanted to be part of their wild club, and even though she felt true, terrier dread, she took a step forward into the tunnel.

First one paw, then another, sank into the grit. She moved with her ears flattened against her head, panting with anxiety. Moonlight glinted off the corrugated metal and Velvet saw shapes materialize in the reflections as she walked: a running cat, a bird in flight, a rubber ball. As her body flooded with fear, the reflections began to get weirder. They were fractured and bowed and filled with images of dogs. There were dogs she'd sniffed, dogs she'd yowled at from the car, dogs she'd humped in alleys or hoped to hump.

As she pressed ahead, dogs that she'd never seen in her life began to emerge. She saw terriers, gloomy and indistinct, with coats like wire and piercing barks. Their tails were up in the air and they were digging. Digging! They dug for rats or badgers or snakes, for foxes or gophers or squirrels. How did she know? She just *knew*. She watched the terriers dig with purpose and a magnificent, terrier zeal. They burrowed toward things with soft bellies that squeaked in holes, they burrowed toward things that emitted the urine of fear, and when they finally got deep enough to reach the little fuckers, they tore at them with their gleaming teeth.

Velvet was in the middle of the tunnel at this point, with a tube of darkness extending ahead of her and behind. There she was, a spayed girl and a knee-licker, seeing the kind of freaky visionary stuff very few pets ever get to see. She was afraid, she was shaking, but she plodded on, determined to transcend her little yard and her festooned ears and the pasty meat crackers that arrived at the same time every afternoon. The farther she journeyed into the tunnel, the more contempt she had for all of that stuff—petting and food bowls and chew treats and kisses—and the more she felt herself part of the breeders, the hunters, the throat-ripping killers.

When Velvet came out at the far end, the coyote lying in wait lunged forward and took a chunk out of her flank. Velvet turned around and ran back through the tunnel, she went running, running, running back through the desert and over the stinky knoll, past the old poodle and the lizard under the rock, through the streets and up the driveway and into her little yard (the gate had been left open for her when she went missing). She made straight for the sliding glass door and threw herself against it again and again, smearing it with blood. The family was in the other room watching TV, but eventually the girl got up to put her ice-cream bowl in the sink; when she saw the shock of red glowing against the glass she screamed first, then dropped the bowl for good measure.

The girl was still trembling when she wrapped Velvet in a towel and lifted her into the car. Her mother drove them to the emergency veterinary clinic, where Velvet was stabilized and stitched up and tranquilized and threaded to an IV, which dripped an infusion of thawed dog blood and saline into a vein in her shaved paw.

When she woke up two days later she was at home, inside a cardboard box. Around her neck was a plastic hood that prevented her from seeing, sniffing, or licking any part of her lower body. After turning in circles for an hour, Velvet sank down on her unbitten side. She lay there, listening to the sound of her breathing amplified inside the hood.

Velvet recovered and sort of forgot about the incident, though when the coyotes howled at night she paced the grass or licked her side, rotating through pangs of longing and sadness and joy. Something had changed. Though she couldn't remember exactly how it had happened, she knew that she'd become one of them, a wild thing, a humping, blood-drinking beast. Moments came when she was filled with elation, pride in her instincts, knowledge of her supremacy, though at other times—when the leash jerked, when she was shoved from a chair—she plunged into a shadowy heartache that displayed itself as a fit of coughing, followed by obsessive paw licking.

Years passed. The girl left for college and Velvet got too old to hurl herself at the door. During a cold snap, the mistress of the house took pity on Velvet and allowed her to come inside for a while. The dog was surprisingly good, quiet and well behaved, following the mistress from room to room and gazing up at her with cavernous eyes. After that, she was allowed into the house on a regular basis. Why not? The mistress had fewer duties since the children had left and she liked being accompanied by a creature who needed her, yet could be locked in the garage at a moment's notice (this was rarely necessary). In time, the mistress found herself becoming attached to Velvet. She spoke to her in a soft voice and gave her treats from a canister; she petted her head and brushed her coat. "Good girl," she said, and meant it. "Good girl."

Velvet, in turn, slept at her feet or sniffed her pants. Escape no longer intrigued her. Her joints hurt and she had plenty of indoor interests, anyway: smelling, eating, self-licking. At night she slept in a little straw basket in the kitchen. It was a good spot, the epicenter of dropped scraps. She didn't want to go outside anymore. She wanted to be in. Still, when she stared out the window, something nagged her. Wasn't there something out there? Something of great consequence? But Velvet was a dog who could only think of one thing at a time (tops); it was her habit to go from a

smell to a sound and back again, which left her largely free
from introspection. Yet she lingered at the window, staring.

The mistress began to bring her along on errands, lifting
her into the car and settling her on the passenger seat for
the journey. When the mistress arrived at her destination,
she tucked Velvet's body under her arm and took her inside
with her, or let her trot along at her heels. In the post office
and in shops and on sidewalks, women stopped in their
tracks to coo at Velvet. "Isn't she cute?" they exclaimed. "Isn't
she sweet?" Velvet looked up and sniffed their hems. She
wagged her tail and licked their fingers.

The mistress often mused, while lifting her into the car
or stroking her Brillo-pad ears, that there was nothing special about Velvet. She wasn't particularly smart or cute or
charming, really. Given a chance—this had actually happened—she'd eat cat shit out of a litter box without hesita-
tion. Their mutual affection had emerged only after years,
when the dog was too tired for bad behavior, and there was
something devious about this. Still, Velvet was a good girl,
calm and sweet, trailing the mistress up and down the stairs
despite her arthritis. The mistress spent so much time in her
company that she felt peculiar without her, lonely and
dazed, and as a consequence they spent very little time
apart. Each day, she rattled the canister of treats and said, "I
love you, Velvet. Yes I do."

Velvet became tubby and gave up barking and forgot
about dogs. She no longer mixed with other dogs or
dreamed of mixing with dogs. In a sense, she'd become
something else, a dog/doll/baby carried from place to place,

where she could be endlessly petted and admired. When she barked, she barked in rounds of three: *I—Am—A*... In her free time, she sauntered from one comfortable spot in the house to the next; when she arrived, she collapsed on her side with a groan. Before she fell asleep, the little hairs over her eyes trembled as she gazed up at a world that had begun, at this late date, to give her an abundance of love.

One day when the mistress got out of bed, instead of prancing around with excitement, Velvet stayed glued to the carpet, staring up at her with listless eyes. It was all downhill after that. She lay in her straw basket for weeks, half comatose, though she could be convinced to get up now and then to eat a cube of cheese. The veterinarian who examined her explained that there was nothing she could do. Her little liver was failing and she was an old girl, very old. She might linger on, it was fine as long as she seemed comfortable, but she was nearing the end. Velvet gave the vet a glance, then rested her head on her paws. She was tired, and her stomach felt as though it were filled with rocks.

A month later, when even the smelliest cheese couldn't rouse her from the floor, the mistress bundled Velvet in a towel and took her back to the vet's office. The doctor gave her an injection, and as Velvet began to wilt in her mistress's arms, she was flooded with visions once again—all around her, above and below, she saw dogs. They were jumping and peeing, they were humping and digging. She'd almost forgotten, but now she remembered: dogs! There were dogs she'd sniffed and dogs who were strangers, good dogs who retrieved and better dogs (far better) who dug for rats. Then, beyond that, she saw the best dogs of all: wild dogs that howled and mated, killer dogs with sloping tails who went for the throat. The knowledge flooded back to her: this was her true pack. These were her brothers and sisters, the bad dogs, the ones who craved blood, who rolled in it. Velvet had learned only one thing in her entire life (since no one had ever tried to teach her anything else), and so she left this world absolutely sure of what she was: a wild thing, a feral, throat-ripping beast.

In the arms of her weeping mistress, Velvet growled. Then she twitched once and died.

THE CAVEMEN IN THE HEDGES

There are cavemen in the hedges again. I take the pellet gun from the rack beside the door and go out back and try to run them off. These cavemen are tough sons of bitches who are impervious to pain, but they love anything shiny, so I load the gun up with golden Mardi Gras beads my girlfriend Kim keeps in a bowl on the dresser and aim toward their ankles. There are two of them, hairy and squat, grunting around inside a privet hedge I have harassed with great labor into a series of rectilinear shapes. It takes the cavemen a while to register the beads. It's said that they have poor eyesight, and of all the bullshit printed in the papers about the cavemen in the past few months, this at least seems to be true. They crash through the branches, doing something distasteful. Maybe they're eating garbage. After a while they notice the beads and crawl out, covered in leaves, and start loping after them. They chase them down the alley, occasionally scooping up a few and whining to each other in that high-pitched way they have when they get excited, like little kids complaining.

I take a few steps off the edge of the patio and aim toward the Anderson's lot. The cavemen scramble after the beads, their matted backs receding into the distance.

"What is it?" Kim stands behind me and touches my arm. She's been staying indoors a lot lately, working on the house, keeping to herself. She hasn't said so, but it's pretty obvious the cavemen scare her.

"A couple of furry motherfuckers."

"I think they are," she says.

"What?"

"Mother fuckers. Without taboos. It's disgusting." She shivers and turns back inside.

After scanning the treetops, I follow. There haven't been any climbers reported so far, but they are nothing if not unpredictable. Inside, I find Kim sitting on the kitchen floor, arranging our spices alphabetically. She's transferring them out of their grocery store bottles and into nicer ones, plain glass, neatly labeled. Kim has been tirelessly arranging things for the last four years—first the contents of our apartment on Pine Avenue, then, as her interior decorating business took off, other people's places, and lately our own house, since we took the plunge and bought it together last September. She finishes with fenugreek and picks up the galanga.

I go to the living room and put on some music. It's a nice, warm Saturday and if it weren't for the cavemen, we'd probably be spending it outdoors.

"Did you lock it?"

I tell her yes. I get a beer from the fridge and watch her. She's up to Greek seasoning. Her slim back is tense under her stretchy black top. The music kicks in and we don't say much for a few minutes. The band is Milk Makes Mucus, and they're singing: *Everyone is dancing out of control!* We used to be punk rockers, Kim and I, back in the day. Now we are homeowners. When the kids down the street throw loud parties, we immediately dial 911.

"The thing that gets me," I say, "is how puny they are."

"What do they want?" asks Kim. Her hair is springing out of its plastic clamp, and she looks as if she's going to cry. "What the fuck do they want with us?"

When the cavemen first appeared, they were assumed to be homeless examples of modern man. But it soon became obvious that even the most broken-down and mentally ill homeless guy wasn't *this* hairy. Or naked, hammer-browed, and short. And they didn't rummage through garbage cans and trash piles with an insatiable desire for spherical, shiny objects, empty shampoo bottles, and foam packing peanuts.

A reporter from KUTA had a hunch and sent a paleontologist from the U out to do a little fieldwork. For some reason, I was watching the local news that night, and I remember this guy—typical academic, bad haircut, bad teeth—holding something in a takeout box. He said it was *scat*. Just when you think the news can't get any more absurd, there's a guy on TV, holding a turd in his hands, telling you the hairy people scurrying around the bike paths and Dumpsters of our fair burg are probably Neanderthal, from the Middle Paleolithic period, and that they have been surviving on a diet of pizza crusts, unchewed insects, and pigeon eggs.

People started calling them cavemen, though they were both male and female and tended to live in culverts, heavy brush, and freeway underpasses rather than caves. Or they lived wherever—they turned up in weird places. The security guard at the Ice-O-Plex heard an eerie yipping one night. He flipped on the lights and found a half dozen of them sliding around the rink like otters. At least we knew another thing about them. They loved ice.

Facts about the cavemen have been difficult to establish. It is unclear if they're protected by the law. It is unclear if they are responsible for their actions. It *has* been determined that they're a nuisance to property and a threat to themselves. They will break into cars and climb fences to gain access to swimming pools, where they drop to all fours to drink. They will snatch food out of trucks or bins and eat out of trash cans. They avoid modern man as a general rule but are becoming bolder by the hour. The university students attempting to study them have had difficulties, though the kids have managed to discover that the lugs cannot be taught or tamed and are extremely difficult to contain. They're strong for their size. It's hard to hurt them, but they're simple to distract. They love pink plastic figurines and all things little-girl pretty. They love products perfumed with synthetic woodsy or herbal scents. You can shoot at them with rubber bullets all day and they'll just stand there, scratching their asses, but if you wave a little bottle of Barbie bubble bath in front of them, they'll follow you around like a dog. They do not understand deterrence. They understand desire.

Fathers, lock up your daughters.

Kim sits across from me at the table, fingering the stem of her wineglass and giving me the Look. She gets the Look whenever I confess that I'm not ready to get married yet. The Look is a peculiar expression, pained and brave, as if Kim has swallowed a bee but isn't going to let on.

"It's fine," she says. "It's not like I'm all goddamn *ready*, either."

I drain my glass and sigh. Tonight she's made a fennel-basil lasagna, lit candles, and scratched the price tag off the wine. Kim and I have been together for ten years, since we were twenty-three, and she's still a real firecracker, brainy, blond, and bitchy. What I have in Kim is one of those cute little women with a swishy ponytail who cuts people off in traffic while swearing like a marine. She's a fierce one, grinding her teeth all night long, grimly determined, though the object of her determination is usually vague or unclear. I've never wanted anyone else. And I've followed her instructions. I've nested. I mean, we bought a house together. We're co-borrowers on a thirty-year mortgage. Isn't that commitment enough?

Oh no, I can see it is not. She shoots me the Look a couple more times and begins grabbing dishes off the table and piling them in the sink. Kim wants the whole ordeal: a white dress, bridesmaids stuffed into taffeta, a soft rain of cherry blossoms. I want none of it. The whole idea of marriage makes me want to pull a dry-cleaning bag over my head. I miss our punk rock days, Kim and me and our loser friends playing in bands, hawking spit at guys in BMWs, shooting drugs and living in basements with anarchy tattoos poking through the rips in our clothing. Those times are gone, and we've since established real credit ratings, I had the Circle A tattoo lasered off my neck, but … but … I feel as though marriage would exterminate the last shred of the rebel in me. For some reason, I think of marriage as a living death.

Or, I don't know, maybe I'm just a typical guy, don't want to pay for the cow if I can get the milk for free.

Kim is leaning in the open doorway, gazing out at the street, sucking on a cigarette. She doesn't smoke much anymore, but every time I tell her I'm not ready, she rips through a pack in a day and a half. "Those creatures would probably wander in and ruin a wedding, anyway," she says, watching a trio of cavemen out on the street, loping along, sniffing the sidewalk. They fan out and then move back together to briefly touch one another's ragged, dirty-brown fur with their noses. The one on the end, lighter boned with small, pale breasts poking out of her chest hair, stops dead in her tracks and begins making a cooing sound at the sky. It must be a full moon. Then she squats and pees a silver puddle onto the road.

Kim stares at her. She forgets to take a drag, and ash builds on the end of her cigarette. I know my girlfriend; I know what she's thinking. She's picturing hordes of cavemen crashing the reception, grabbing canapés with their fists, rubbing their crotches against the floral arrangements. That would never do. She's too much of a perfectionist to ever allow that.

When I first saw the cavemen scurrying around town, I have to admit I was horrified. It was like when kids started to wear those huge pants—I couldn't get used to it, I couldn't get over the shock. But now I have hopes Kim will let the marriage idea slide for a while. For this reason, I am somewhat grateful to the cavemen.

It rains for three days and the railroad underpasses flood. The washes are all running, and on the news there are shots of SUVs bobbing in the current because some idiot ignored the Do Not Enter When Flooded sign and tried to gun it through four feet of rushing water. A lot of cavemen have been driven out of their nests, and the incident level is way up. They roam around the city hungry and disoriented. We keep the doors locked at all times. Kim has a few stashes of sample-size shampoo bottles around the house. She says she'll toss them out like trick or treat candy if any cavemen come around hassling her. So far, we haven't had any trouble.

Our neighbors, the Schaefers, haven't been so lucky. Kim invites them over for dinner one night, even though she knows I can't stand them. The Schaefers are these lonely, New Age hippies who are always staggering toward us with eager, too-friendly looks on their faces, arms outstretched, as if they're going to grab our necks and start sucking. I beg Kim not to invite them, but at this stage in the game, she seems to relish annoying me. They arrive dressed in gauzy robes. It turns out Winsome has made us a hammock out of hemp in a grasping attempt to secure our friendship. I tell her it's terrific and take it into the spare room, where I stuff it in a closet, fully aware that by morning all our coats are going to smell like bong water.

When I return, everyone is sipping wine in the living room while the storm wets down the windows. Winsome is describing how she found a dead cavebaby in their back yard.

"It must not have been there for long," she says, her huge eyes welling up with tears, "because it just looked like it was sleeping, and it wasn't very stiff. Its mother had wrapped it in tinsel, like for Christmas."

"Ick," says Kim, "how can you cry for those things?"

"It looked so vulnerable." Winsome leans forward and touches Kim's knee. "I sensed it had a spirit. I mean, they're human or protohuman or whatever."

"I don't care," says Kim, "I think they're disgusting."

"Isn't that kind of judgmental?"

"I think we should try to understand them," chimes in Evan, smoothing down his smock—every inch the soulful, sandal-wearing, sensitive man. "In a sense, they're us. If we understood why that female caveman wrapped her baby in tinsel, perhaps we'd know a little more about ourselves."

"I don't see why people can't just say 'cavewoman,'" snaps Kim. "'Female caveman' is weird, like 'male nurse.' Besides, they are *not* us. We're supposed to have won. You know, survival of the fittest."

"It might be that it's time we expanded our definition of *humanity*," intones Evan. "It might be that it's time we welcome all creatures on Planet Earth."

I'm so incredibly annoyed by Evan that I have to go into the bathroom and splash cold water on my face. When I get back, Kim has herded the Schaefers into the dining room, where she proceeds to serve us a deluxe vegetarian feast: little kabobs of tofu skewered along with baby turnips, green beans, rice, and steamed leaf of something or other. Everything is lovely, symmetrical, and delicious, as always. The house looks great. Kim has cleaned and polished and organized the contents of each room until it's like living in a furniture store. The Schaefers praise everything and Kim grumbles her thanks. The thing about Kim is she's a wonderful cook, a great creator of ambiance, but she has a habit of getting annoyed with her guests, as if no one could ever be grateful enough for her efforts. We drain a couple more bottles of wine and after a while I notice that Kim has become fed up with the Schaefers, too. She starts giving them the Look.

"Seriously," she begins, "do you two even like being married?"

They exchange a glance.

"No, c'mon, really. It's overrated, right?" Kim pulls the hair off her face and I can see how flushed she is, how infuriated. "I think all that crap about biological clocks and baby lust, it's all sexist propaganda meant to keep women in line."

"Well, I haven't noticed any conspiracy," offers Winsome, checking everyone's face to make sure she's not somehow being disagreeable. "I think marriage is just part of the journey."

"Ha," says Kim. "Ha, ha, ha." She leans across the table, swaying slightly. "I know," she pronounces, "that you don't believe that hippie shit. I can tell," she whispers, "how fucking lost you really are."

Then she stands, picks up her glass, and weaves toward the back door. "I have to go check the basement."

We stare at the space where Kim was for a while. Winsome is blinking rapidly and Evan keeps clearing his throat. I explain we have an unfinished basement that's been known to fill with water when it rains, and that the only entrance to it is outside in the yard, and that Kim probably wants to make sure that everything's okay down there. They nod vigorously. I can tell they're itching to purify our home with sticks of burning sage.

While Kim is gone I take them into the living room and show them my collection of LPs. I pull out my rare purple vinyl X-Ray Specs record, and after considering this awhile, Winsome informs me that purple is a healing color. We hear a couple of bangs under the house. I toy with the idea of checking on Kim, but then I recall the early days of our courtship, before all this house-beautiful crap, when Kim used to hang out the window of my 1956 hearse, which was also purple, and scream "Anarchy now!" and "Destroy!" while lobbing rocks through smoked-glass windows into corporate lobbies. It's difficult to worry about a girl like that.

It doesn't take long for the Schaefers and me to run out of small talk. I have no idea how to get them to go home; social transitions are Kim's jurisdiction. We sit there nodding at each other like idiots until Kim finally straggles back inside. She's muddy, soaked to the bone, and strangely jolly. She says there's about a foot of water in the basement and that she was walking around in there and it's like a big honking wading pool. She giggles. The Schaefers stare with horror at the puddle spreading around her feet onto our nice oak floors. I put my arm around her and kiss her hair. She smells like wet dog.

———

I come home from work a few days later and find Kim unloading a Toys "R" Us bag. I notice a diamond tiara-and-necklace set with huge, divorcée-size fake jewels stuck to a panel of pink cardboard. Again, she seems happy, which is odd for Kim. In fact, she's taken to singing around the house in this new style where she doesn't sing actual words, she goes, "nar nar nar," like some demented little kid. It drives me crazy, in particular when the game is on, so I tell her to fucking please cut it out. She glares at me and storms off into the back yard. I let her pout for a while, but I'm in the mood to make an effort, so I eventually go out and find her standing on a chair, hanging over the hedge, gazing at the alley. I lean in beside her and see a caveman shambling off with a red bandana tied around his neck, like a puppy.

"That's weird."

"Look at his butt."

I look. There's a big blob of pink bubble gum stuck in his fur.

"God," says Kim, "isn't that pitiful?"

I ask her what we're having for dinner. She looks at me blankly and says, I don't know what are we having for dinner. I tell her I'll cook, and when I get back from picking up the pizza, she's nowhere to be found. I walk from one empty room to another while the hairs on my arms start to tingle. I have to say, there's a peculiar feeling building in the household. Things are in a state of slight disarray. There's a candy bar wrapper on the coffee table, and the bag from the toy store is on the kitchen floor. I yell Kim's name. When she doesn't appear, I turn on the TV and eat a few slices straight from the box. For some reason, this starts to bother me, so I get up and get a plate, silverware, and a paper napkin. Kim walks in a little while later. She's wet from the waist down and all flushed, as if she's been doing calisthenics.

"I was bailing out the basement!" she says, with great verve, like basement bailing is a terrific new sport. Her hair is tangled around her head and she's sucking on a strand of it. She is smiling away. She says, "I'm worried about letting all that water just stand down there!"

But she doesn't look worried.

———

On the news one night, a psychic with a flashlight shining up under his chin explains there's a time portal in the condemned Pizza Hut by the freeway. Though the mayor

whines he wasn't elected to buckle to the whim of every
nutbar with an opinion, there are televised protests featur-
ing people shaking placards proclaiming the Pizza Hut
ground zero of unnatural evil and finally they just bulldoze
it to shut everyone up. A while after that, the incident lev-
els start to drop. It seems that the cavemen are thinning
out. They are not brainy enough for our world, and they
can't stop extinguishing themselves. They tumble into
swimming pools and drown. They walk through plate glass
windows and sever their arteries. They fall asleep under
eighteen-wheelers and wander onto runways and get
mauled by pit bulls.

It looks as if we're the dominant species after all; rock
smashes scissors, *Homo sapiens sapiens* kicks *Homo sapiens
neanderthalensis*'s ass.

As the caveman population drops, the ominous feeling
around town begins to lift. You can feel it in the air: women
jog by themselves instead of in pairs. People barbecue large
cuts of meat at dusk. The cavemen, it seems, are thinning
out everywhere except around our house. I come home from
work and walk through the living room and peek out the
back window just in time to see a tough, furry leg disappear
through a hole in the hedge. The hole is new. When I go
outside and kick around in the landscaping, I find neat little
stashes of rhinestones and fake pearls, Barbie shoes, and
folded squares of foil wrapping paper. The cavemen can't see
that well, but have the ears of a dog and flee as soon as I rus-
tle the window shades, but one time I peel back the shade
silently and catch a pair skipping in circles around the

clothesline. One of them is gripping something purple and hairy, and when I go out there later I find a soiled My Little Pony doll on the ground. They are not living up to their reputation as club-swinging brutes. More than anything, they resemble feral little girls.

Also, our house has become an unbelievable mess. Kim walks through the door and drops the mail on the coffee table, where it remains for days until I remove it. There are panties on the bathroom floor and water glasses on top of the television and scraps of food on the kitchen counter. When I ask Kim what's going on, she just says she's sick of that anal constant housekeeping bullshit, and if I want it clean, I can clean it myself. She looks straight at me and says this, without flinching, without any signs of deference or anger or subtle backing away that had always let me know, in nonverbal but gratifying ways, that I had the upper hand in the relationship. She tosses an orange peel on the table before marching outside and descending into the basement.

I stand there in the kitchen, which smells like sour milk, shaking my head and trying to face up to the increasingly obvious fact that my girlfriend of ten years is having an affair, and that her lover is a Neanderthal man from the Pleistocene era. They rendezvous in our moldy, water-stained basement, where he takes her on the cement floor beneath a canopy of spider webs, grunting over her with his animal-like body, or perhaps behind her, so that when she comes back inside the house, there are thick, dark hairs stuck all over her shirt and she smells like a cross between some musky, woodland animal gland and Herbal Essences shampoo. Furthermore, she's stopped shaving her legs.

The next day, I duck out of the office claiming I have a doctor's appointment and zip back home around noon. I open the door with my key and creep inside. I don't know what I'm looking for. I think I half expect to find Kim in bed with one of those things, and that he'll pop up and start "trying to reason" with me in a British accent. What I find instead is an empty house. Kim's car is gone. I poke around, stepping over mounds of dirty clothes, then head out back and take the stairs to the basement. When I pull the door open, the first thing to hit me is the smell of mold and earth. I pace from one side to the other and shine my flashlight around, but I don't see anything suspicious, just an old metal weight-lifting bench with a plastic bucket sitting on top. Maybe, I think, I'm making this whole thing up in my head. Maybe Kim just goes down there because she needs some time to herself.

But then on my way out, I spot something. On the concrete wall beside the door, several feet up, my flashlight picks out a pattern of crude lines. They appear to have been made with charcoal or maybe some type of crayon. When I take a few steps back, I can see it's a drawing, a cave painting of some sort. It's red and black with the occasional pompon of dripping orange that looks as if it were made by someone who doesn't understand spray paint.

I stand there for two or three minutes trying to figure out what the painting is about, then spend another fifteen trying to convince myself that my interpretation is wrong. The picture shows half a dozen cars in a V-shaped formation bearing down on a group of cavemen. The cavemen's flailing limbs suggest flight or panic; obviously, the figures are in danger of being flattened by the cars. Above them, sketched in a swift, forceful manner, floats a huge, godlike figure with very long arms. One arm cradles the fleeing cavemen while the other blocks the cars. This figure is flowing and graceful and has a big ponytail sprouting from the top of her head. Of course it's meant to be Kim. Who else?

———

I go upstairs and sit at the kitchen table, elbowing away half a moldy cantaloupe, and hold my head in my hands. I was hoping it was nothing—a casual flirtation at most—but a guy who makes a cave painting for a girl is probably in love with the girl. And girls love to be loved, even high-strung ones like Kim. I admit I'm hurt, but my hurt switches to anger and my anger to resolve. I can fight this thing. I can win her back. I know her; I know what to do.

I put on rubber gloves and start cleaning everything, thoroughly and with strong-smelling products, the way Kim likes things cleaned. I do the laundry and iron our shirts and line everything up neatly in the closet. I get down on my knees and wipe the baseboards, then up on a chair to dust the lightbulbs. I pull a long clot of hair out of the drain. There's a picture of us in Mexico in a silver frame on top of the medicine cabinet. I pick it up and think, That is my woman! It's civilization versus base instinct, and I vow to deploy the strongest weapon at my disposal: my evolution-arily superior traits. I will use my patience, my facility with machinery and tools, my complex problem-solving skills. I will bathe often and floss my teeth. I will cook with gas.

A little after five, Kim walks in and drops the mail on the coffee table. She looks around the house, at the gleaming neatness, smiling slightly and going "nar nar nar" to the tune of "Nobody Does It Better." I stand there in my cleanest suit with my arms hanging at my sides and gaze at her, in her lit-tle professional outfit, pretty and sexy in an I-don't-know-it-but-I-do way, clutching her black purse, her hair pulled back with one of those fabric hair things.

"God, I can't believe you cleaned," she says, and walks through the kitchen and out of the house into the yard and slams the basement door behind her.

———

Kim is so happy. The worst part is she's so disgustingly happy and I could never make her happy all by myself and I don't particularly like her this way. For a couple of weeks she walks around in a delirious haze. She spins around on the porch with her head thrown back and comments on the shape of the clouds. She asks why haven't I bothered to take in the pretty, pretty sunset, all blue and gold. Like I fucking care, I say, forgetting my pledge to be civil. It's as though someone has dumped a bottle of pancake syrup over her head—she has no nastiness left, no edge, no resentment.

Her hair is hanging loose and she has dirty feet and bad breath. She smiles all the time. This is not the girl I originally took up with.

Of course, I'm heartsick; I'm torn up inside. Even so, I do my best to act all patient and evolutionarily superior. I keep the house clean enough to lick. I start to cook elaborate meals the minute I get home from work. I groom myself until I'm sleek as a goddamn seal. I aim for a Fred Astaire/James Bond hybrid: smooth, sophisticated, oozing suaveness around the collar and cuffs—the kind of guy who would never fart in front of a woman, at least not audibly. She has a big, inarticulate lug already. I want to provide her with an option.

Kim takes it all for granted, coming and going as she pleases, wandering away from the house without explanation, hanging out in the basement with the door locked, and brushing off my questions about what the hell she's doing down there, and with whom. She doesn't listen when I talk to her and eats standing up in front of the refrigerator with the door open, yelling between bites that it's time for me to go to the store and get more milk. One evening I watch her polish off a plate of appetizers I have made for her, melon balls wrapped in prosciutto, downing them one after another like airline peanuts. When she's finished, she unbuttons the top button of her pants and ambles out the door and lets it slam without so much as a glance back at me. Without so much as a thank you.

I trot out after her, figuring it's about time I give her a suave, patient lecture, but I'm not fast enough and she slams the basement door in my face. I pound and scream for a while before giving up and going up into the yard to wait. The night is very still. There's a full moon and the hedges glow silver on the top and then fade to blue at the bottom. I get a glass of iced tea and pull a chair off the patio, thinking to myself that she can't stay down there forever. I think about how maybe I'll catch the caveguy when he comes out, too. Maybe I can tie on an apron and offer them both baby wieners on a toothpick.

After a while I hear a rustling in the hedges. At that moment I'm too miserable to be aware of the specifics of what's going on around me, so I'm startled as hell when a cavegirl pops out of the hedge, backlit in the moonlight, and begins walking toward me with a slow, hesitant gate. I sit there, taking shallow breaths, not sure whether I should be afraid. She has a low brow and a tucked, abbreviated chin, like Don Knotts's, but her limbs are long and sinewy. When she gets closer I see that she looks a lot stronger than a human woman does, and of course she's naked. Her breasts are like perfect human pinup breasts with bunny fur growing all over them. I can't unstick my eyes from them as they bob toward me, moving closer, until they come to a stop less than an arm's length from my chin. They are simultaneously furry and plump and I really want to bite them. But not hard.

She leans in closer. I hold very still as she reaches out with a leathery hand and begins to stroke my lapel. She lowers her head to my neck and sniffs. On the exhale, I discover that cavegirl breath smells just like moss. She prods me a few times with her fingertips; after she's had enough of that she just rubs the fabric of my suit and sniffs my neck while sort of kneading me rhythmically, like a purring cat. It's obvious she likes my suit—a shiny, sharkskin number I've hauled out of the back of the closet in the interest of wooing Kim—and I guess she likes my cologne, too. For a minute I feel special and chosen, but then it occurs to me that there's something sleazy and impersonal about her attention. I'm probably just a giant, shiny, sandalwood scented object to her. The moon is behind her so I can't see her that clearly, but then she shifts and I get a better view of her face and I realize she's young. Really young. I feel like a creep for wanting to feel her up, more because she's about fourteen than because she's Neanderthal.

She swings a leg over and settles her rump onto my thigh, lap-dance-style.

I say, "Whoa there, Jailbait."

The cavegirl leaps up like she's spring-loaded. She stops a few feet away and stares at me. I stare back. She tilts her head from side to side in puzzlement. The moon shines down. I reach into my glass and draw out a crescent-shaped piece of ice, moving with aching slowness, and offer it to her on a flat palm. She considers this ice cube for a good long time. I hold my arm as still as possible while freezing water trickles off my elbow and my muscles start to seize. Then, after a few false lunges, she snatches it from my hand.

"Nar," she says. Just that. Then she darts back into the hedge with her prize.

I remain in the moonlight for a while, shaking with excitement. I feel almost high. It's like I've touched a wild animal; I've communicated with it—an animal that's somehow human, somehow like me. I'm totally giddy.

This is probably how it was with Kim and her guy when they first met.

━━━━

I guess I'm a complete failure with every category of female because the cavegirl does not come back. Even worse, Kim continues to treat me as if I'm invisible. It's painfully clear that my strategy of suaveness isn't working. So I say screw evolution. What's it ever done for me? I go out drinking with the guys and allow the house to return to a state of nature. The plates in the sink turn brown. I shower every other day, every third. Kim and I go days without speaking to each other. By this time there are hardly any cavemen left around town; the count is running at one or two dozen. I go to the bars and everyone is lounging with their drinks all relaxed and relieved that the cavemen aren't really an issue anymore, while I continue to stew in my own miserable interspecies soap opera. I don't even want to talk to anyone about it. What could I say? Hey buddy, did I mention my girlfriend has thrown me over for the Missing Link? It's humiliating.

One hungover afternoon, I decide to skip the bars and come straight home from the office. Kim, naturally, is not around, though this barely registers. I've lost interest in tracking her whereabouts. But when I go into the kitchen, I catch sight of her through the window, standing outside, leaning against the chinaberry tree. She looks sick or something. She's trying to hold herself up but keeps doubling over anyway. I go outside and find her braced against the tree, sobbing from deep in her belly while a string of snot swings from her nose. She's pale and spongy and smudged with dirt and I get the feeling she's been standing there crying all afternoon. She's clutching something. A red bandana. So it was him. The one with gum on his butt.

"Where is he?"

"He's gone," she whispers, and gives me a sad, dramatic, miniseries smile. "They're all gone."

Her sobs begin anew. I pat her on the back.

So she's curled over crying and I'm patting her thinking, well, well, now that the other boyfriend is gone she's all mine again. Immediately, I'm looking forward to putting the whole caveman ordeal behind us and having a regular life like we had before. I see all sorts of normal activities looming in the distance like a mirage, including things we always made fun of, like procreating and playing golf. She blows her nose in the bandana. I put my arm around her. She doesn't shake it off.

I should wait, I know, I should go slow; but I can see the opening, the niche all vacant and waiting for me. I feel absolutely compelled to exploit it right away, before some other guy does. I turn to Kim and say, "Babe, let's just forget about this whole caveman thing and go back to the way it was before. I'm willing to forgive you. Let's have a normal life without any weird creatures in it, okay?"

She's still hiccupping and wiping her nose but I observe a knot of tension building in her shoulders, the little wrinkles

of a glare starting around the edge of her eyes. I realize I'm
in grave danger of eliciting the Look. It dawns on me that
my strategy is a failure and I'd better think fast. So I bow to
the inevitable. I've always known I couldn't put it off forever.

I take a deep breath and drop to one knee and tell her I
love her and I can't live without her and beg her to marry me
while kissing her hand. She's hiccupping and trying to pull
her hand away, but in the back of my mind I'm convinced
that this is going to work and of course she'll say yes. I've
never made an effort like this before; I've only told her I love
her two or three times total, in my life. It's inconceivable
that I won't be rewarded. Plus, I know her. She lives for this.
This is exactly what she wants.

I look up at her from my kneeling position. Her hair is
greasy and her face is smeared with dirt and snot, but she's
stopped crying. I see that she has created a new Look. It in-
volves a shaking of the head while simultaneously pushing
the lips outward, like she's crushed a wasp between her teeth
and is about to spit it out. It's a look of pity, pity mixed with
superiority; pity mixed with superiority and blended with
dislike.

"I don't want a normal life without any creatures in it,"
Kim says, her voice ragged from crying, but contemptuous
nonetheless. "I want an extraordinary life, with everything
in it."

The Look fades. She brings her dirty, snotty face to mine
and kisses me on the forehead and turns and walks away,
leaving me on my knees. I stumble into the house after her. I
can smell a trail of scent where she's passed by, cinnamon

and sweat and fabric softener, but though I run through the house after her, and out into the street, I don't see her anywhere, not all night. Not the night after that. Never again.

———————

Some psychic with a towel on his head says the cavemen passed through his drive-through palm-reading joint on their way back to the Pleistocene era, and I finally go over and ask him if he saw Kim with them. He has me write him a check and then says, "Oh *yeah*, I did see her! She was at the front of this line of female cavemen and she was all festooned with beads and tinsel, like she was some sort of goddess!" He says it in this bullshit way, but after some reflection I decide even charlatans may see strange and wondrous things, as we all had during the time the cavemen were with us, and then report them so that they sound like a totally improbable lie.

It's bizarre, the way time changes things. Now that the cavemen are gone, it seems obvious that their arrival was the kind of astonishing event people measure their entire lives by. And now that Kim is gone, it seems clear that she was astonishing, too, regal and proud, just as she's represented in the cave painting. I once thought of her as sort of a burden, a pain-in-the-ass responsibility, but now I think of her as the one good thing I had in my life, an intense woman with great reserves of strength, forever vanished.

Or, I don't know; maybe I'm just a typical guy, don't know what I have until it walks out on me.

I've been trying to get over her, but I can't stop wallowing in it. One night we hold a drum circle on the site of the old Pizza Hut, and I swear that after this night, I'll force myself to stop thinking about her. This drum circle is the largest yet, maybe a couple of hundred people milling around, having the kind of conversations people have these days—you know, we were annoyed and frightened by the cavemen when they were here, but now that they're gone we just want them back, we want that weird, vivid feeling, the newness of the primitive world, and so on. My job is to tend the fire. There's a six-foot pyramid of split pine in the middle of the circle, ready to go. At the signal, I throw on a match. The wood is soaked in lighter fluid and goes up with a whoosh. Everyone starts to bang on drums, or garbage can lids, or whatever percussive dingus is handy, while I stand there poking the flames, periodically squirting in plumes of lighter fluid, as the participants wail and drum and cry and dance.

We are supposedly honoring the cavemen with this activity, but in truth no one ever saw the cavemen making fires or dancing or playing any sort of musical instrument. Apparently, the original Neanderthal did these things; they also ate one another's brains and worshipped the skulls of bears, though no one seems anxious to resurrect these particular hobbies. Still, I admit I get kind of into it. Standing there in the middle, sweating, with the sound of the drumming surrounding me while the fire crackles and pops, it's easy to zone out. For a moment I imagine what it might be like to live in an uncivilized haze of sweat and hunger and fear and desire, to never plan, to never speak or think in words—but then the smell of lighter fluid snaps me back to how artificial this whole drum circle is, how prearranged and ignited with gas.

Later, when the fire has burnt out, some New Age hardcores roll around in the ashes and pray for the cavemen to come back, our savage brothers, our hairy predecessors, and so on, but of course the cavemen don't come back. Those guys look stupid, covered in ash. When the sun comes up, everyone straggles away. I get into my hatchback and listen to bad news on the radio as I drive home.

THE LONG HALL

It's so boring where we live that a certain percentage of high schoolers have gone completely berserk—late-night partying, stupid driving, sex antics, smoking, and drinking—a lot of kids are doing it, not just Shane and me. My theory is that Utah's purity deranges people. It's common to see women floating around downtown dressed like prairie wives, lifting their ankle-long skirts to swirl across perfectly clean sidewalks. Temple Square looks as if it's scrubbed down at night by elves, and everywhere you go, you see big families walking around together, happy as larks. It's enough to turn anyone into a swearing, drugged dissident. But when we first moved here, I thought this was the most beautiful place in the world. We had our house in the pines with the mountains rising around us, and because of a proclamation by Brigham Young, all the streets had to be wide enough to turn a wagon around in. Everyone was so friendly, always smiling and offering us ice cream and candy. Now I realize that people's teeth are rotting in their mouths and that you have to run across the intersections to make it before the light changes. Worst of all, half the pines are dying or dead from the effects of the drought and the ensuing infestation of bark beetles. First the needles turn rust-red, then brown. Finally they wither into dry, crackling sticks.

"Beetling is natural," says Mr. Clark, our revolting neighbor. I'm strapped into the passenger seat of his LTD, trying not to focus on his blown-dry hair. Lately I've been getting into his car when I hitchhike, even though Mr. Clark speaks in a monotone and has no spark. He's like a burned-out lightbulb. Plus, he's a pervert.

"The beetles take the sick, the old, the weak," he drones. "Healthy trees survive."

"Yeah, but Mr. Clark, *all* the trees are dying."

"Beetling is natural," he insists.

Mr. Clark is *old*. He's wearing a flowered shirt. There's sweat on his upper lip and his car smells like disinfectant. Once, I opened up the glove compartment and it was full of little packets called Wet Naps.

"'Natural' means sun, air, water, sexual intercourse," he says, gesturing at the world outside the car. "Trees are part of nature. They can't all be dying. Believe me, young lady. That's impossible."

"The newspaper said some forests south of here are a hundred percent dead."

"Newspapers lie."

"What? They do not."

He slows the car and turns to me. "Who are you going to trust? Me or some stupid newspaper reporter?"

I cross my arms and turn to stare out the window. There's a big spruce outside my room, and sometimes an owl roosts there and makes a beautiful hooting sound. I check the tree daily for the first sign of death—a purple tinge at the end of the branches or weeping holes in the bark. I can't lose that tree. It rustles in the wind and lulls me to sleep at night.

Mr. Clark stops the LTD a few houses from mine, beside a lot of dying piñon pines—they're mostly brown, still hanging on, but barely. I grab the handle and pull but Mr. Clark has his thumb on the power locks. I try to look at his face without actually looking at his eyes. "Thanks for the ride."

"You're very welcome." Mr. Clark slides his hand up my leg.

"God, that's just so gross."

Mr. Clark leans toward me. "There's nothing gross about the human body."

"You know what? I'm fourteen, and you're disgusting."

Mr. Clark looks at me with his mean, football coach face and says, "You poor child. Next time I'll leave you at the bottom of the hill." Then he releases the locks.

I scoot across the vinyl and fly out the door. I lied. Actually, I'm fifteen.

———

I keep promising my sister, Shane, that I won't hitchhike but Shane has been out a lot, doing her senior year things. She's there when I get home, though, putting dishes in the dishwasher. She looks at my bag from CD Outpost and says, "Don't take rides from strangers."

"I know."

"Don't take rides from Mr. Clark."

"That jackanapes," adds my mother.

Shane looks at me. "Seriously. He's a dick wad. I'll kick his ass."

She would, too. Shane has toughness down to a science—she's aloof and laconic and exactly like James Dean would have been if James Dean had been a girl. She's got that slow burn inside her; it's magnetic. Really. People stop talking when she walks into a room.

"I'll take you next time," my mother says. "I'll *pilot* you!"

Shane and I look at each other and smirk.

That night I lie in bed and listen to my new CDs. I like a lot of new stuff and also really old rock and roll—Elvis, the Kinks, the Pretenders—whatever makes me feel like I'm going to live forever or else just curl up into a ball and die. I can hear my tree between the songs, rustling in the wind. There's already one beetle hole in the bark, dripping sap.

———

It's not just the trees; other things have been deteriorating around here. My sister's friend Morgana, for instance, mutated into a girly girl overnight. Before that, she was Shane's disciple. She had the same chopped-up hair and the same hands-in-pocket slouch and poker face—no smiles, no makeup—and stood behind Shane plunking on her bass when their band practiced in the basement rec room. This seemed fitting, since Shane practically created Morgana. She gave her her name, saving her from a lifetime's worth of

Tiffany Ann. "That's not a human name," Shane told her, "that's a cat's name."

Then one day Morgana waltzes into our house and sits on the couch and starts talking to my *mother*. Nobody talks to my mother. "How are you, Mrs. Audrey," and "You're looking lovely today, Mrs. Audrey." She has her hair smoothed down with little flowered clips and she's wearing nail polish and glitter eye shadow and the kind of stretchy pants everyone wears at the mall. My mother pushes her braids behind her ears and takes off her reading glasses.

"You're not my daughter."

"No. I'm Morgana."

"Well, Morgana," my mother locates her glass of wine, "why don't you shut your fucking trap?"

Morgana's eyes widen. "Excuse me?"

"You heard me, little faker. Rotten little charlatan."

Morgana rockets off the couch and heads downstairs. I follow, sliding over the steps in my socks. Shane is already there putting a new string on her Stratocaster or something. Morgana walks into the middle of the rec room and stands there, hands on her hips, posing.

"My God, your mother is such a bitch."

Shane barely reacts—she just lets her eyelashes slide down a notch over her pupils. Shane is sort of short and has big brown eyes and a pointy little nose, like Bambi, but it doesn't matter. She looks tough, anyway.

"What the fuck is wrong with you?"

"Not one little thing."

"What are you wearing?"

"Clothing," replies Morgana.

"You're shitting me."

"I shit you not."

Shane continues giving Morgana a cool, flat look. "There's no way you can be a Pep Pill and look like that."

"Okay, fine. Then I'm not a Pep Pill."

"Good. You always were our weak link."

"That's because the bass is for fucking losers."

"Then you've been a fucking loser for three years straight, *Tiffany Ann*."

"I can't wait to get out of here," Morgana sputters, scooping up some pieces of lint from the floor—I guess they belong to her. She opens the back door and says, "I'm going to go to *college*," before she slams it.

Shane finishes stringing her guitar. Then she ambles over and picks up Morgana's bass and hands it to me. "You better start practicing," she says.

"Wait," I say. The bass is heavy.

"For what?"

Every afternoon that week, Shane has me stand by the amplifier and practice my bass lines and it's *loud*: A A A A, G G G G. She explains about four-four time and how to shove the little ands between the numbers and how to come down heavy on the *one*. I understand what she's saying, but man, I suck.

"You totally suck," Shane agrees. Still, Paula shows up and she's banging on the drums and we run through "Boys Are Bad News" nine times while Shane asks me if my fingers are bleeding yet. "I want to see blood on the fret board RIGHT NOW!" she says, and then that becomes a new song ("Blood on the Fret Board") and we play that, and I still suck.

"Shane," I finally say, "I have to go do my homework."

Her whole face stays still but she raises one eyebrow. "Homework," she says, "is for pussies."

Eventually this becomes one of my all-time favorite songs by the Pep Pills: "Homework Is for Pussies." Shane says since I brought up homework, I can be considered the coauthor of the song. I shrug and say, "Cool," but on the inside I'm jumping up and down. I can't believe it. I'm going to be a rock star just like my sister.

<hr/>

You'd never know it now, but when we first moved to Utah we were almost like a normal family. The only odd thing about us was the crazy-earth-religion thing. My parents had a pile of worn-out paperbacks sitting on the coffee table; the one on top said: *How To Be Your Own Shaman.* They liked to wear feathered headbands and meet other shamans on the rocks in Monument Valley to feel the earth's energy converge. Sometimes they would take us along. Shane and I used to sit in the backseat on the long drive and make up jokes. (How many shamans does it take to change a lightbulb, none, they're already enlightened, etc.) If we weren't doing that, then on Wednesday and Saturday nights they made us go to the Church of Gail, where the energy of the natural world is harvested. A bunch of members used to circle their hands over Harmony Wong's head with the intention of straightening her crossed eye. They did this on and off for about a year until my father packed up and left and my mother started to buy wine in cardboard boxes.

It's really not so bad having a wino mother, once you get used to it. There are plenty of comical aspects—pratfalls, insults slurred at telemarketers, absurdities uttered in a drunken rage—and other benefits, like a total lack of adult supervision. It's true that it can also be a problem, but we try to manage this by charting my mother's drinking schedule and adjusting our routine to fit it. Every day, it's basically the same. In the morning, she's seminormal. She sits at the table drinking coffee and tells us to leave her alone. Sometimes she runs some errands and comes back with a few groceries and a couple boxes of burgundy with a pour spout at the bottom. To lend seriousness to these expeditions, she sits in the kitchen and jots notes on a pad that says *Things to Get* (on which Shane once wrote "a life").

Later, when we arrive home from school, she's usually dressed and parked in her leather chair, watching TV and doing crosswords. She stays there all afternoon, glazing the rim of her wineglass with lipstick, her long, gray braids hanging down in front of her shoulders and her squash blossom necklace clamped around her neck—staring at the TV, staring out the window, staring at nothing, looking like a faded, dissolute version of a Navajo wise woman. This is when she likes to call me sweetie and if I let her she'll tell endless stories about my adorable infancy. We usually try to stay in the basement then, though we can often get things from her at this point—the car keys, for instance. "The kissy-kissy stage," Shane calls it. "Followed by the enraged, abusive stage."

That comes around nightfall. It's usually preceded by an introductory period, like the aura before a migraine, when my mother adopts a vaguely British accent and starts yelling at us in a strange, huffy vocabulary. She says stuff like "That haughty little miss can just march upstairs and pack her valise!" or "You two spoiled brats think life is one big bildungsroman—well it's not!" This level of drunkenness is hazardous because she's not too wasted to throw stuff at us, and we find it hard not to laugh when she flings around words like *motorcoach* and *hausfrau*. ("Do you think I wanted to spend my whole life as some spavined old hausfrau hauling her kids around in a motorcoach?") I've spent many afternoons giggling in the hallway with the dictionary, dodging projectiles.

By eight or nine o'clock she's slurring her words and saying we ruined her life, us and our cad of a father; her eyes are weeping and bloodshot and she's incredibly mad but also nodding off during the dramatic pauses. This is a good time to stay away from her, but if I get cornered, I end up hearing about the things she could have been. She could have been a great attorney, with her brilliant legal mind, or a horse trainer, or a traditional healer, or a decorator; of course I try to slink off, like the ungrateful slattern I am. Stop right there, she slurs, fingering her squash blossom necklace like a weapon. She could have been a philanthropist (trampolinist?)

or a hand model or a lady senator or a great spiritual leader like Mary Baker Eddy.

"Look at this hand," she thrusts it under the lamp. It's mottled, with chewed-down nails, and she's still wearing her wedding ring even though my father has long since gotten hitched to Montana or Dakota or whatever her name is—the fat girl from the Church of Gail. "It was so white and smooth, like porcelain—listen! Don't you turn your back on me! French porcelain—I had the French ambassador tell me so himself. *Limoges*!"

This often goes on until Shane grabs me by the shoulders and steers me up the stairs and into my room.

"It didn't seem like she even loved him that much when he was still around," I say. "I don't see why his leaving made her into such a raging drunkard."

Shane sits on the foot of my bed with her legs crossed. "Yeah."

"What's her problem?"

"Who knows. The world is fucked. Men make women into pathetic weaklings," Shane flips her bangs over her eyes. "My motto is Stay independent."

"I know. Mine, too."

"They're pretty much all jerks, on some level." Shane has said this a lot since my dad left. "What level isn't always obvious. Some guys are okay to pal around with. I just don't trust them."

I say I don't, either.

There was a time right after my dad left when I did not yet think he was such a jerk. I remember I helped him pack all his stuff into a big, rented truck while my mother locked herself in the bedroom. When all his camping gear and weight sets and new-age workbooks were shoved inside and he was ready to hit the road, he sat down next to me on the curb and put his arm around me. "Well, kiddo," he said, "it's going to be a long haul."

I was only about eleven and I thought he said a long *hall*. I pictured a hallway lined with open doors. My father and I were poised at the entrance, ready to walk the long hall together.

It's been four letters, two phone calls, and three years since any of us have seen him. Shane says he sends child support checks in envelopes with his lawyer's return address on them. And that she'd kill him if she thought he was worth it.

———

Anyway, Morgana comes over almost every day, even though she and Shane are still in a big fight. "I left a Donnas CD here somewhere," she says, or, "I have to check and see if my bass is okay."

"Take it home," Shane says.

"I can't. My brothers will trash it."

I'm pretty sure Morgana's brothers are away on their church missions, but I don't mention it, because Morgana is teaching me her parts to all the Pep Pill songs, and besides, I don't think Shane really cares. Morgana just likes to hang out at our house; everybody does. My mother never comes downstairs no matter how much noise we make or what we burn in the fireplace—once, the dining room chairs—and one night we all stood in the driveway and threw our empty beer bottles against the house, one by one, in the order in which they were drained. My mother stayed upstairs, sleeping or passed out. So it's pretty much a free-for-all around here.

I still can't get used to Morgana's new look. She's become a half-Morgana, half-prom-queen chimera who sounds like Morgana and chain smokes like Morgana, but who wears little froufrou outfits and a gold ankle bracelet that says *delicious*. There's also perfume and lip gloss and a velvet purse with a gold drawstring. Shane stands there in her old jeans, with her keys attached to her belt loop with a chain, and just shakes her head. Or she'll brush past Morgana and say, "Excuse me, Princess, can you move your butt?" which I like, or, "Excuse me, Princess Delicious," which I like even better and try to convince Shane to make into a song. She tells me I should write it myself.

When Shane goes upstairs, Morgana grabs my arm and pulls me into the corner. She puts her face next to mine. It smells like a wet ashtray.

"There's still time to grow this out." Morgana lifts a chunk of my hair and examines the roots.

"What are you talking about?"

"You still have a chance to be pretty," Morgana whispers, "don't let *her* screw it up. Your hair could be completely blond again by your senior year. Do you know what that means?"

"I like it black."

"Listen to me: you have a cute face. Your legs are flexible. You could be a cheerleader."

"Morgana, that's revolting."

"Pay attention, Christie," she digs her nails into my arm. "Rebels don't get anywhere. Not once high school is over. They put makeup over their tattoos and get jobs as supermarket cashiers."

"I'm going to tour with the Pep Pills."

"Right," smirks Morgana. "Just remember, cashiers who don't kiss ass are the first ones replaced by self-checkout machines."

I watch Morgana's lip gloss glittering in the light from the wall sconce. She's a mystery to me. The Pep Pills have always been about nongirly toughness, that Joan Jett/Pat Benatar/Chrissie Hynde thing, three-chord rock and roll, no bullshit, no complications. I don't get it. Why would anyone want to give that up?

After she leaves, I write this:

> *Princess Delicious with her snotty pink airs*
> *Princess Delicious with dumb bows in her hair*
> *Yeah, yeah, I'm suspicious*
> *That Princess Delicious*
> *Thinks she's too good to do the dishes . . .*

And then I can't think of anything else.

If that's not weird enough, the next thing that happens is Morgana shows up one day with a boy. Just a boy in itself—that's not alarming. But *this* boy is really fucking cute, and not clean-cut cute, either, like Mormon boys, who tend to look like future TV weathermen. This boy's skin is super, super pale, almost blue, and he looks *dirty*. Dirt under his nails, frayed, grease-stained jeans on his tall, nearly gaunt body, mud on his cuffs, and on his front pocket, an ink stain, black and heart-shaped. I look at him and say a little prayer: God, let there be a black stain on his skin underneath, too. Morgana leads him into the rec room and flops down on the futon couch. The boy crosses his arms and rests his foot against the wall.

"This is Johnny," she says. "He moved here from New York."

"Hi," Johnny mumbles, and half-smiles. My mouth must be hanging open. He looks at me for a second, and in that second, I notice that he has light blue eyes with a dark ring around the outside. His hair is thick and almost black, with comb marks at the temples. I can't speak. All I can think is *Elvis*. A skinny, soiled, bluish Elvis.

I look over at Shane. Her mouth is open too. She does something I've never seen her do before: she raises her hand and tucks a little strand of hair behind her ear. Then she lowers her eyes and says, "Hey."

"Do you guys ever use this pool table?" Johnny ambles toward the table and leans into it with one hip.

"Sometimes," Shane says. Obviously not lately. There are cords and CDs and books strewn all over the felt.

"Mind if I play?"

"Of course not." Shane slings her guitar behind her and begins moving the crap off the pool table.

Johnny racks up the balls; Shane doesn't even say anything, she just grabs a cue and starts grinding it into a cube of chalk. Johnny breaks—a fast break that scatters the balls but doesn't sink any. Shane steps up to the table. When she lowers the cue I see that her hands are shaking, slightly. The guitar is still slung over her back. She hits one ball in, then another. We've had that pool table ever since we moved, since before Shane started the Pep Pills. During her freshman year, she used to come home after school every day and shoot pool until midnight. It's the kind of thing she's really good at. I've seen Shane sink every ball without once missing. She eases a bumper shot into the corner.

"Nice," Johnny says, and squats down, holding on to his stick.

Naturally, she beats the pants off him.

He doesn't say anything. Shane just raises one eyebrow and stands there while he racks the balls.

She beats him again. They switch to nine ball. Morgana and I slink around, dodging their cue sticks, putting CDs on the boom box, and getting sodas out of the fridge.

"You're wiping the floor with me," Johnny finally admits. Shane looks right at him and smiles. *Smiles*—this is Shane I'm talking about. Johnny looks at her and smiles back. I'm sitting all the way over on the stairs, and *I* can feel the electricity zinging between them.

That's when Morgana says, "I'm playing winner," from her spot on the futon couch. We all turn and stare, as though it's a big shock that she's still there.

Shane wins, of course. Morgana gets up in her little skirt and lip gloss with her diet soda in one hand and the stick in the other. She makes a few lame attempts at sinking a ball. When she shoots, her tongue creeps out of her mouth. Finally, she turns to Johnny and says, "Help me!"

"Okay," he says, "you have to square your hips." He places his hands on either side of Morgana's body and gently adjusts her stance. I can't believe it. I can't believe Johnny is touching Morgana. I look over at Shane and she's leaning against the wall with no expression on her face, but she's gripping the cue stick so hard I can see the veins sticking out of her hand.

Morgana hits the ball and it slides into the pocket.

"That felt good," she purrs.

Personally, I'd like to kill her.

Morgana misses the next shot and Shane steps up to the table. Her hands aren't shaking anymore. She hits all the balls in one long run, and she hits them really hard. We all stand there watching, listening to the balls going *thwack* into the pockets. In some way I can't quite explain, it's as if we're watching her do something more violent than hitting balls with a stick. It's like watching her slaughter an animal.

When it's all over, Morgana says, "Good game." Shane gives her a blank stare. Morgana clasps her hands behind her back so her boobs stick out. "I wish I could do something really well, like be a pool shark." She turns to Johnny and takes his hand. "Are you ready to leave?"

In my opinion, Johnny doesn't look ready to leave. He's holding on to Morgana but his body is tilted toward Shane. Still, he says, "I guess."

"Good." Morgana gets up on her tiptoes and kisses him on the *mouth*. She turns and tows him toward the door.

"See you guys later." That's it. Johnny turns and leaves.

After he's gone, Shane runs into the bathroom and locks the door. I knock but she won't open it. I can hear her keening, "Oh my God, oh my God," like Brianna Peterson, the hall monitor, did once after Brian Owens, the star quarterback, put his arm around her.

So I'm pretty sure that life as I know it is over.

———

I should probably mention that around this time, I find this letter in my mother's handwriting, lying under some mail on the kitchen counter.

Dear Eugene,

How are you? I hope you're having a wonderful time ~~canoodling with~~ fucking that horse-faced child you bamboozled into the institution of matrimony. I'm sure you thank the Earth Goddess every day for the hallowed gift of Viagra to help you keep it "up." I hope also that you delight in spending the money that ought to be going to your wonderful, intelligent, and talented daughters. They are doing just dandy without you, or any word from you, though Shane is probably a lesbian due to the psychic wound you have bestowed on her.

Re: your remarriage: I hope that when you vowed to love and cherish that bedraggled child, she reminded you that you also promised the same things to me before abandoning me in this vulgar dwelling like the lump of excrement you are. Just the other day, I went to the drugstore and saw dear Mrs. Chaplan, our neighbor. She had her hip replaced but is up and about now. She said to tell you to go fuck yourself and so did your old golf buddy Dr. Pfefferson when I saw him a couple of years ago. He said: "Tell that old scoundrel to go fuck himself." So, I thought I'd pass that on.

I have given some thought to your proposal and have concluded that we do not wish to be graced by your presence at the end of the month, as you have proposed. DO NOT COME HERE. I asked the girls if they wanted to see their father and they said, "Father? Who is our father? We have no father. We are fatherless children." If you come, they'll just be confused. Haven't you done enough harm?

Your wife,
Peggy

We start practicing more, harder; I'm learning new songs almost every day. The Pills played out a lot before Morgana quit, sometimes at parties, sometimes at an all-ages venue called Astro Dome Stadium, a storefront way west on 2nd South that hosts a variety of diversions, including wrestling, possibly cockfighting, and, on Tuesday nights, square dancing. There are bleachers on three sides and a stage with a chain-link fence around it. The fence is fun because you can climb on it like a monkey. The plan is for us to play a gig there as soon as I'm good enough.

"Shane, I think I'm ready."

Shane just stares at me—she rubs her tongue behind her teeth, her Bambi eyelashes whooshing up and down when she blinks, until I say, "What?"

"Christie, you're holding your bass upside down."

Okay, that's true, but even so, I'm actually getting a little better. Shane always says that the bass is easy. Once I get calluses on my left hand, the only hard part is remembering songs, and there are so many Pep Pill songs. Shane is a song factory—she has a huge notebook full of them. I know a bunch now, including some of my favorites: "Your Rules Suck," "No Never Not," "The I Don't Dance Dance," "Babies Are Ugly," "Take a Pep Pill (and Call Me in the Morning)." We practice almost every day that Paula doesn't have marching band. Sometimes Morgana shows up and sulks around. She slouches on the couch and smokes cigarettes, two things she's forbidden to do at home.

"What's Johnny doing?" I ask.

"Homework or something. He's taking me to a movie later."

I glance at Shane and she's *blushing*. My sister blushing, hell freezing over, my mother quitting the sauce—just a few things I never thought I'd witness in my lifetime. Morgana has been smart enough not to bring Johnny around again, but I do see him at school sometimes, walking through the halls in his unclean clothes, dragging a pen against the lockers so it goes *tock tock tock*. He always says hello to me. He's a new kid; this alone is enough to ward most people off, not to mention his dirty-gaunt-blue aspect. Usually he's alone or with Morgana, but one time I came out of Biology, and he and Shane were talking in the parking lot. They both turned to me and said, "Hi, Christie," and it was weird—I felt really happy. I felt like they were my parents.

"I got accepted to Pepperdine," Morgana says, lighting a new cigarette with the cherry of her last one, "but I don't have to decide for another month."

"That's terrific," Shane says, with no expression on her face. Shane didn't apply anywhere. She always says, "Rockers don't do college."

"I'm probably going to get into a lot of schools," Morgana continues. She exhales smoke through her nose in a snort, like a dragon. "My parents are already panicking—we'll miss you, Tiffany Ann, what will we do without you, Tiffany Ann, what can we buy you, Tiffany Ann. You know how it is."

Shane gives her the Shane stare—blank, one eyebrow cocked, slow blinks.

"Well, anyway, Christie knows how it is. Right?"

"No."

"Leave her alone," says Shane.

"What? What did I say?"

"Don't be a cunt," Shane says.

Morgana looks stricken; the C-word is too much for her. The color drains from her face. Then she rallies and blurts, "You should talk, dyke."

Shane and I lose it—we both start laughing hysterically like we used to during moments of reflection at the Church of Gail. Morgana glares at us, then screws up her mouth and sticks another cigarette in it. Shane and I are stumbling over and I inhale some spit so my laughing turns into a coughing fit. And that is when, for the first time in four years of partying, band practice, and prolonged antics with firecrackers, we hear my mother's voice descending from the top of the stairwell.

"Girls! Girls!"

"Mom?"

"You girls shut up down there!" Her voice changes, as though she's already turned away, but we hear her say, "I'm not running a burlesque house."

It takes me a while, but I finally figure out that I have rhythm. Of course I have rhythm. How could I have less rhythm than Princess Delicious? I can play the bass line to "Take a Pep Pill" perfectly, which is good enough, Shane says, for the Astro Dome Stadium. We sign up to play on a bill with four other bands. All we have to do is load up the Volvo and roll it down the hill for a few yards before Shane starts the engine—I don't know if this is even necessary. My mother has never said anything when we take the car without permission. But something inside us, some latent good-girl instinct, pushes us to be crafty about it.

When we get to the Astro Dome, we drive around to the back and start unloading our equipment, trying to keep our cables from dragging in the oil leaking from the Dumpster the taco stand uses. By eleven there will be tons of kids here, but we're on first, so it's still relatively empty. The Astro Dome is just a concrete hall with metal shades covering the windows and rows of fluorescent lights buzzing on the ceiling. A few clumps of kids are clustered here and there, holding skateboards and talking. Truthfully, it seems more likely that a game of bingo will break out than rock and roll. Even so, there's sweat running down my sides and I feel horribly nervous and sick.

"What if I throw up?"

Shane crouches over an amplifier and looks at me. "Really?"

"Yeah. What if I pee in my pants? What if I start to scream uncontrollably?"

Shane tilts her head. "I don't see a problem with that."

"Shane!"

"No, I'm serious. Any of those options is just going to increase your punk rock credentials."

Johnny walks up to the chain-link fence and climbs it partway. He hangs there with his arms stretched above his head so we can all see his beautiful biceps. Something about him looks different—more intense and moody. I think he's dyed his eyebrows black.

"Hey," Johnny says, and looks in Shane's direction, then up at the ceiling.

"Hey," Shane replies, and scratches her neck.

Johnny pops off the fence and circles back into the bleachers while Shane grips the neck of her guitar with a pained expression on her face.

I say, "You should tell him."

Shane looks at me with her big doe eyes glazed over like dried sap and says, "Just shut up."

By the time we start to play, a few more kids have begun skulking around or climbing up on the bleachers—mostly, though, I try not to look at the people. I look at my hands or I look at Shane, who's singing with her mouth touching the microphone. I'm trying to play right, but I have an unhealthy, spelling-bee feeling. C C C C, D D D D—aren't those the right letters? Maybe it's okay; Shane seems to be singing and Paula seems to be hitting the drums. I try to play in time. I try to listen when Paula clicks her sticks together at the beginning of each song. This is the best moment—right before the music starts, before we've had a chance to fuck anything up.

When it's over, we immediately load the equipment back into the car so that no one will steal it. I have so much adrenaline buzzing in my ears that I sort of don't remember playing and I definitely don't remember going back inside until I'm sitting on the bleachers rubbing my shoe against the metal planks and Johnny is there, sitting beside me.

"That sounded pretty good."

"Oh man, I sucked."

"No, not really."

"I sucked royal."

"I don't know. I couldn't hear it. Maybe you sucked in a good way."

I try to look at Johnny but I can't; he's too cute. If I look at him I'll start to laugh or cry.

"Wanna go get some beer?" he asks.

I say sure and follow him out to his Honda. I feel better outside—it's a windy spring night with just a few spots of snow left in the gutters and under cars. Johnny starts the Honda and pulls out into the avenue in a wobbly arc. I fasten my seat belt. I guess he didn't drive much back in New York.

"I don't know why Morgana quit," he says. "Your band is cool."

I tell him I don't know why either.

We drive for a while without talking, then he says, "Shane seems like kind of a loner. Does she hang out with anyone?" He does a weird brow furrow. It looks like he's been practicing it.

"She hangs out with the band."

He clears his throat. "No, I mean, does she have a boyfriend?"

I think for a second and then say, "Not at the moment."

Johnny parks in the Albertsons lot. You can't buy wine or hard liquor in grocery stores in Utah, but you can buy beer—I mean, if you're twenty-one you can. I have no idea what Johnny is planning to do. He grabs a cart and starts wheeling it down an aisle. He takes some pickles from the shelf. He tosses some cling peaches and candied yams into the basket. The way he lopes across the tile floor, shoulders rolled back, his long legs swinging, makes my stomach drop. He slows down in the cereal section. He puts his hands on his hips and nods toward the shelves. "Which of these seems the least like food?" he asks.

I have to weigh my options, but finally I point to something called Frosty Blue Cupcakes. He throws it in the cart.

We round the corner and wheel down a few more aisles; at some point a couple of six-packs get tossed into the cart, but we just keep going, past the paper products, into the baking aisle.

"Hey, look at these." Johnny holds up a package of birthday candles.

"What about them?"

He takes a step toward me. Then he takes another step. He's so close to me that I can smell Johnny and Johnny smells like pine needles and Jergens lotion. The blue ring around his iris flushes darker as he approaches me. I know that if he keeps looking at me this intensely I'm going to start to cry. My eyes are already welling up when I feel his hand snake under my jacket. He's grabbing the waistband of my jeans.

"Christie," he says, "this is going to be cold." Then he shoves a can of beer down my pants.

We fit two more beers into my pants and four into Johnny's. He puts a couple more inside his jacket and leaves the rest in the cart. We keep wheeling through the store, picking out a few more items (votive candles, hemorrhoid cream), until we abandon the cart in the pharmacy and stroll out through the automatic doors. So, Johnny's a thief. A shoplifter. I think this would make a great Pep Pills song: *Johnny is a thief / And he stole my heart / He tossed it in a bag / In the Super Kmart*, except Shane hasn't been writing any songs about Johnny. In fact, ever since she met him, I've noticed that Shane hasn't been writing any new songs, period.

After that, we just drive around for a while. I suppose we're heading back to the Astro Dome, but Johnny takes the scenic route and I feel really happy just being his passenger. The snow is melting off the mountains, the night smells like mud, and in the dark after some beer, you can't tell that all the trees are dying. Johnny wedges a beer can between his legs and it pokes up from his crotch in a fascinating way. Shane would probably not be confused by this. On the floor on my side of the car there's a red sweater that must be Morgana's. I think about Morgana and how I used to really like her, but now I hate her, and I'm comforted by the thought that she'll leave for college in the fall.

"Hey Johnny," I say, "what are you doing after you graduate?"

He turns up the radio. "I love this song!"

"Are you going to work in a garage?" This strikes me as a fitting job for Johnny. He could spend all day getting his hands even dirtier.

"A garage?"

"Or go to college?"

"Uh, no. Not right away."

"What then?"

Johnny presses his lips together. "I'm going away." He takes a swig of beer.

"You are? I don't think you should do that."

"I kind of have to."

"Why? Where are you going?"

He pauses, and then he says, "I don't know."

"How can you not know?"

He takes another swallow of beer and stares straight ahead. "I'm going on a mission."

I scream, "No!"—it just sort of escapes. I clamp my hand over my mouth, stunned. A mission—that's for good Mormon boys. They become missionaries for two years after high school and get sent anywhere on the planet; they're marooned there with a partner and the Book of Mormon, and can only make two phone calls a year—to their family—one on Christmas and one on Mother's Day. So Johnny will be gone, profoundly gone.

Plus—he's a good Mormon boy?

Johnny looks over at me and his face softens. "It seems kind of bizarre, I know. But I can't stay here."

"Shane is staying."

"Oh yeah?" Johnny nods and looks away.

"Anyway, if she went somewhere, I'd have to go with her. Because of, you know, the thing with my mother."

"What thing is that?"

"Morgana didn't tell you?"

"No."

I really, truly do not want to tell Johnny about our crazy mother, but the words just roll out of my mouth. "She's a frothing wino. We're waiting for her to hit rock bottom. Ha, ha," I laugh, because I'm used to laughing about my mother. Since having an alcoholic mother is a big joke.

We've stopped at a red light. Johnny looks over at me and doesn't laugh. He looks concerned, sad, something along those lines. "That's not good," he says. He reaches into his jacket and hands me another beer.

We drive back to the Astro Dome in silence. I squeeze my hands together, trying to imprint this feeling. Being with Johnny, he's just so cute, so cool, so nice, there's no way to describe it. It's like this wrenching and beautiful experience. The only thing I can compare it to is the part of "Heartbreak Hotel" where you can barely hear Elvis, his voice has sunk to such a low, sexy sob, and he sings: *I get so lonely, I get so lonely baby, I get so lonely I could die.*

────────

I guess I'm drunk, but I don't see why this matters, since I've been drunk plenty of times before. Still, when I get back in the car with Shane, she's annoyed. My feet are in the cup holder, and Shane keeps telling me to take them out and sit up and put on my seat belt. All these seat belts—there's Johnny's seat belt and Mr. Clark's seat belt and the Volvo's seat belt, and on some level they're all fundamentally futile.

Shane zips up her jacket and squints through her bangs. "Will you stop making that noise?"

"No."

"Christie, what's your problem?"

"You have to tell him."

Shane sighs. Paula is gone. Someone must have given her a ride. We're sitting in the parking lot with the engine running and the heat on. Shane keeps checking the rearview mirror. "I don't want to talk about this."

"You have to tell him how you feel."

"He likes Morgana."

"Morgana's an idiot. Besides, I think he likes you."

"Then why can't he say something?"

"Because he's a pussy."

"I have no use for pussies."

"Shane," I snap my fingers, as though that's going to help, "you *have* to tell him. You have to tell him because he doesn't know. You're graduating and he's going away and you'll never see him again and you'll go to your grave without ever kissing him, or touching his skin, or telling him that you're in love with him."

"He's going away?"

"He's going on a *mission*."

"Oh man." She punches the dashboard. "Fuck."

"Yeah, I know."

"Fuck. Fucking fuck."

"I know."

"Shit."

"You have to *say* something to him."

"Oh man." Shane turns to look at me and sort of collapses forward on the steering wheel. The horn blares and keeps blaring like it does in the movies when the driver gets shot. I don't think Shane even hears it; she looks exhausted, as if she's caught some sickness, and it occurs to me that she might love Johnny almost as much as I do.

———

I think we just feel and feel and feel as children, or as kids or whatever, and then at some point, we get older and have to decide how much to feel, because it's too arduous to go through *that* every day—it's just too much, like listening to heavy metal nonstop. There's a line you step across, a deal you make with yourself. I was going to watch Shane do it, and I would copy her, and then everything would be okay for me. My tree would thrive. The drought would be over.

That was my *plan*.

Anyway, one day we're lurking in the basement waiting for Paula to show up, when we hear a car roll to a stop in the driveway. We expect Paula to knock on the basement door but instead the bell rings, and since my mother is too saturated to even get out of her chair, I go upstairs to answer it. To my surprise, when I open the door, my dad is standing on the stoop jangling his keys. My *father*. There's something on his face—a goatee—and his hair is really short. He looks familiar but also strange, like a cross between Concert Date Ken and my dad.

"Hello, Pumpkin."

"Hi, Dad." I stand there feeling weird.

"Can I come in?"

"Oh, sure." I step aside and let him pass. It's a terrible idea for him to come inside, but what can I do? My mother is sitting in her chair and the sun is almost down, which means we're entering one of her special, scary times.

My dad walks into the living room as if he owns it—I think he still might—and says, "Hello, Peg."

My mother has a crossword book on her lap and her glass beside her. She looks at my father and her mouth springs open—her teeth are stained purplish from wine. Then she presses her hands against the arms of the chair as though she's going to jump up and throttle him, but instead she simply says, "Eugene."

Eugene smiles.

My mother smiles back. I smile, too. We all smile. There's enough tension in the air to snap a twig. But we all just stand there for a while until suddenly my mother springs out of the chair and reaches for *me*. Her braids slap me in the face, and while I'm dealing with that, she wraps one arm around my neck and the other around my waist so that she's holding me in front of her like a shield. My mother is repeating, "Eugene, Eugene, Eugene." Each time she says it, it sounds more like a curse word.

"Lighten up, Peg. I come in peace."

"Peace?" She squeezes my throat. "How dare you waltz into this house and speak of *peace*. How dare you waltz in here, not even dressed! Look at you. You're wearing *dungarees!*"

My father shakes his head. He's loose in the knees, tanned, relaxed. He *is* wearing dungarees, and also a polo shirt. He looks like a man who knows his way around a golf course, a man not easily ruffled.

"You're a cad and a fornicator," say my mother. "You're a knave, a scamp, a scoundrel, a rogue."

"Christ, Peg. What do you do? Sit around with a dictionary?"

I giggle, because that's exactly what she does. She tightens her arm on my neck and backs up. She smells terrible, like baby powder dumped on a moldy orange. I think about kicking her.

"Shut up, Eugene."

My mother pulls me back with a jerk. She ducks behind the curtains that hang over the big picture window but leaves me standing out in front of her. From there, she tries to operate me from behind, like a puppet. "Disloyal, faithless," she shakes my arm at my father. "Did you think I wanted to be *here*, at this point in my life?"

"Listen Peg. Let's be wise. Come out from there."

"Wise? Ha! You *lied*. You said she didn't mean anything. You said we'd talk about it."

"Okay, granted, maybe I did. But how can we talk about it if you're behind the curtain?"

"You are not a wise man!" She points my arm at him. "A shitwad is more like it." She tries to make me give him the finger but grabs my pinkie instead so we stand there giving him the pinkie.

This starts me giggling again, which is bad. I know it's bad because my father says, "Christie, wipe that grin off your face right now."

"What's she doing?" says my mother.

"Oh, just being a kid."

"She thinks life is a flashy soiree. She thinks everything is a big debutante ball."

"Christie," says my dad, in a tone I remember from my childhood, "I don't want you treating this like a joke. Conflict between a man and a woman is solemn business."

By now I'm laughing because I'm half-hysterical, and besides, it's absurd that my *parents* are ganging up on me. I mean, parents? What are parents? I have no parents. I am a parentless child.

"Now you want to be the daddy," says my mother, "after *you* abandoned *us*. Isn't that a pretty pickle?"

"I've never stopped being their father."

"Oh really? Then take her."

My mom launches me toward my dad, who kind of catches me and holds me away, looking at me like I'm a strange little thing. Just for a second. Then he sits down in my mother's chair and sniffs her glass of wine.

"Christ, Peg," he says, "I just wanted to see the girls. Why do you have to ruin everything?"

I turn and see Shane standing on the landing. I don't know how long she's been there, but I feel terrible when I see her because she looks scared, and I can't remember ever seeing Shane looking scared. She walks into the room and takes my hand and leads me away. My father doesn't even look at her. His eldest daughter fails to register.

We go downstairs and open a bag of Nutter Butters and take turns digging the cookies out of the bottom. *Jeopardy!* is on. Alex Trebek is such a snot, acting like he knows all the answers personally, but he doesn't. The only person I could ever imagine possibly knowing all the answers is Shane.

————

A few weeks after my father's visit, Johnny stops by our house to say good-bye. He's leaving sooner than I thought—he has to go to some camp to receive language lessons for his missionary work. He says the church is sending him to Tonga, an island in the South Pacific.

I open the door, but he won't come inside. He just stands on the doorstep hunched over like it's cold, except it's not. I hold on to the knob, staring at a blue vein running through Johnny's temple. I can't open my mouth and I can't stop looking at him; for a while, we're both frozen there in some kind of stand-off. Then I start to cry and I feel really conspicuous and stupid, so I pull the collar of my shirt up over my face.

"It's not that bad," he says. "I can surf in Tonga. They have good waves."

"You don't know how to surf," I moan through my T-shirt.

"Sure I do."

"But you're so—untan."

"That's because I wear sunscreen."

This makes me giggle like a lunatic—I think I'm cracking up. I know I'll be able to escape in a minute because I hear Shane coming down the stairs. Before she gets there, Johnny pokes me on my shoulder and says, "You're going to be a real heartbreaker someday."

"I am? When?"

I go inside while Shane walks him to his car. While she's outside with him I run upstairs to check on my tree. I've found two more beetle holes in the bark, but the tree is still hanging in there, green and fluffy with just a few dead needles. I'm seized by a wave of hope. The thing is, I always thought Shane could have anything in the world. I always thought Shane would tell Johnny she loved him and he'd clasp her to his chest and tell her to wait for him. He'd come back from Tonga in two years, he'd whirl her across the floor, they'd make little rock star babies who crawled across the floor in leather jackets. That's what I thought. I thought life was a flashy soiree. I thought it was a fucking debutante ball.

It's hot here in the summer, and dry. The drought has been going on for so long it feels like it will never rain again. This is a true desert, anyway—the lake is pretty but it's pure brine, and all the green stuff in the valley is irrigated. Lawns, hedges, pines—they're all fed by underground rivers pumped up from under the rocks. It seems amazing that anything can flourish at all here. Still, I look down on the greenery as I hike up the hill, heading home.

My thumb's not out, but Mr. Clark pulls over for me anyway. It's incredibly hot and the LTD is so shiny in the sun that it seems to be melting into the asphalt. I open the door and climb inside, into the weird smell of air freshener. I'm thinking about how, when I came back downstairs that day,

Shane was saying, "I couldn't, I couldn't, I couldn't," and holding her face in her hands as Johnny drove away in his little Honda.

"What do you mean? Did you say *anything* to him?"

She shoved her hands under her armpits. "Yeah. I said, 'Have a nice trip.'"

Then she went into the bathroom and locked the door. I stood there thinking, man, if *Shane* can't do it, well—I could see all the doors closing. I knew I would not be walking down the long hall with a boy at my side. We would not be girls with boys, women with men. We'd turn our backs, we'd walk away. Shane and I would always do whatever it took to stay safe.

Mr. Clark must have been holding his fingers under the air conditioner because they feel like ice as they creep up my leg. They creep and stop, then creep some more. Shane used to say that once girls start letting it be about boys, it's *all* about boys. I think no, yes, whatever, fuck it. I really don't care anymore. I look out the window and think of nothing at all, my mind is totally empty—there's just a fragment of a song winding through it, a little piece that goes: *I get so lonely I could die.*

CHRIST, THEIR LORD

W hat were we thinking? Well, it was June. June! One hundred and eight degrees every day. We had been looking for over six months. The house had a pool. A pool! The sign beside the curb said "reduced." Then there was the adorable 1950s-ness of it—the pink and white tile bathroom, the spangled Formica in the kitchen, the flying-saucer light fixtures. And this business about the tyrannical neighborhood association, about the streets being closed to cars and filled up with hay carts and carolers and schoolchildren and tourists, hay carts loaded with mentally disabled adults bellowing with marvel at the shiny, shiny lights, here in the subdivision of Yuletide Village, which so kindly puts on a display of holiday lights for the community for three weeks every winter—spreading the cheer, spreading it like manure—we thought … What did we think? We thought I could handle it. But Jesus fucking Christ.

Outside in the street, I can hear people caroling—*caroling*, the most odious of verbs. And yet:

> *The Cuervo Gold*
> *The fine Colombian*
> *Make tonight a wonderful thing.*

Trevor loves Christmas. He associates it with huge boxes filled with presents, glazed hams, furry mittens, hypnotic lights, pecan pies made just for him. I associate it with empty passageways in deserted malls where "Jingle Bells" plays over and over, followed by a glockenspiel version in Walgreens and "Deck the Halls" piped in to the parking lot, rendered by chipmunks. Meanwhile, edging in from the side is a memory of my mother sitting me down and instructing me how, as a Jewish child, to properly sing Christmas carols:

> *O come all ye faithful, joyful and triumphant*
> *O come ye, oh come ye to Bethlehem*
> *Come and behold him, born the king of angels*
> *O come let us adore him,*
> *O come let us adore him,*
> *O come let us adore him! Christ* THEIR *lord.*

Something happens to people's brains in the Sun Belt. I believe the constant overload of vitamin D has softened my skull and turned me nice, so that I've started to act like a nice person—though maybe with a little more of it, I will overdose and just come into my own nastiness. For it is innate, at my core. The true flowering of my being is bored and acidic and annoyed with the incredible idiots who surround me, always talking about themselves.

As an antidote I decide to read more great books so that I can keep company with the likes of Shakespeare, Virginia Woolf, Plato, but this time around, Socrates strikes me as repulsive, the kind of man who does not shower, does not cut his toenails, and cannot stop disabusing his neighbors of various innocently held notions. He picks food out of his teeth while explaining exactly how and why his fellow citizens are stupid asses—until finally they get so sick of his shit that they *execute* him.

Obviously, this is somewhat extreme. But killing one's neighbors. Now there's an idea.

———

Next door to the west are Jim and Cindy Nickles. She's a kittenish, fifty-year-old schoolteacher with long legs, dyed hair, and eyes loaded with mascara. I find Cindy's girlishness loathsome—her fakey hostess patter, fluttering lashes, house pride, her complete and utter dedication to the veneer—it's all freakishly like a Cheever story, but without the antique furniture. She talks and talks—the subject is Christmas decorations! Because the bad thing is starting, the very, very bad thing. Her husband, Jim, is handsome yet inert, a chair-sitter. "Jim thinks I'm terrible!" she says. Jim leafs through a magazine. Every now and then, perhaps preemptively, Cindy cries, "Jim, Jim, stop!"

In the first week of December, we enter the casual, laid-back ambit of Christmas hell. The neighborhood-wide decorations go up. The cherry pickers give me hope. They are sort of intriguing, with the men wobbling up there in plastic tubs stringing lights along the branches of the Aleppo pines, big, shaggy yetis that do not evoke the tannenbaum. Then, one by one, our neighbors begin to erect elaborate dioramas in their yards. Apparently, there is a contest. Cindy Nickles rings the doorbell and makes me come out and pretend to admire her Wise Men, which are wooden cutouts, decaying and faded like my mental companion Socrates. For some reason, when I look at them I go into a trance; this reminds me of the experience I had with the dead paloverde beetle under the stairs, three inches long and disgusting, eerily reminiscent of half a baked potato. I couldn't tear my eyes away from it. I just stood there for five minutes, zombied out, staring, thinking, *Ick! Ick! Ick!*

Possibly the pot smoking is not helping things.

———

A few words about Trevor: he is not my husband. We do not plan to marry. We do not plan to reproduce. We keep separate bank accounts, and when we go out to dinner, we ask the server to split the check on two cards. In any other neighborhood, in any other part of our mildly liberal desert town, our relationship would be unremarkable. However, we've masochistically chosen to live in the most conservative subdivision we could find, a little slice of *I Love Lucy* and *Leave It to Beaver*, a relic inhabited by school principals and policemen and old, old ladies, plumbing contractors documenting the evils of fluoridated water, a gnarled minister, people with flagpoles in their lawns and RVs named *Windpasser* or *The Invader* parked in their side yards. We ourselves seem so strange by contrast that the neighbors occasionally walk out of their houses and look at us if we are, for example, out front doing some yard work while wearing black T-shirts and black shoes with headphones attached to our heads. What are we? Satanic fornicating animal mutilators? And then there is the parade of homosexuals and curators and musicians and freelancers and enviro-activists and hunchbacks and dwarves and other unmarried people who occasionally visit us, our friends and acquaintances, degenerates all.

Anyway, Trevor. He is so cute. He has a dent in his chin and curly hair that sits flat against his head, like the marble hair on Michelangelo's *David.* Anyone who can do funny voices like he can deserves a medal. Sometimes I think he would drink fourteen martinis every night if he didn't think it would displease me, but he works hard all day in his little home office, designing Web sites that help people buy important things, like patio-misting systems, and is funny and sweet and only occasionally teases me about the dark hair growing out of the mole on my neck. I'm absolutely certain that he loves me, but sometimes, to make sure, I follow him from room to room like a hungry little dog.

You'd think that the Nickles house would have a nicer Christmas display, as everything else in and around their property is polished and controlled in a manner that makes a person wonder when Jim and Cindy stopped sleeping together. The poodle clip of their hedge, the Tombstone roses twined carefully over the trellis around the door—chuppa style, the style of my people, greedy eaters of borscht and chopped liver, and three slices of rye bread with that—for Jim and Cindy Nickles, everything must be outwardly nice. Must be nice! Of course, there's their thirty-five-year-old son who still lives in the back house, a sort of a converted shed with an air conditioner completely conjoined to the double-brick exterior via rust. I've looked inside: cot, dorm fridge, bong, cable box, a stack of comic books hiding a larger stack of porn. The son himself is as pale as a cave creature, though his palms have a faint orange glow from a diet of processed cheese snacks.

That he is roughly my contemporary disturbs me.

And that together we have been doing some bong hits.

———

I need a special sticker on my car now to get in and out of the neighborhood in the evening. The sticker designates me as an accursed resident of Yuletide Village as I honk and scowl and inch my way at five miles per hour through the smiling and entranced crowds touring the holiday lights, until I manage to terrify a lady in a three-wheeled Handy Cart out of the way and turn into my own driveway—a pool of darkness in a sea of light. For we have no decorations. No crèche, no baby Jesus, no rebellious Star of David. No animatronic carolers jerking to and fro like drunken frat dudes, no Charlie Brown in a snowsuit, nothing to delight children or adults or disabled adults or grandparents or sullen adolescents with creamy, sentimental centers who are not really so tough. What we offer the holiday crowd is this: a little of nothing for no one.

I fiddle with the CD player in the dash. I've been experimenting to see what kind of music cancels out Christmas music. I had hopes for hip-hop and thrash metal, but I've discovered that it's the mellow, pot-smoking music of the seventies that neutralizes merriness best. I sit for a minute in the driveway, cranking it. Steve Miller sings about how some people call him the Space Cowboy. Others call him the Gangster of Love.

As I make my way from the carport to the kitchen door, a random man yells at me. "What kind of a jerk doesn't celebrate Christmas?"

"My kind of jerk," I mutter back.

In the evening, Trevor sits me down. He says he has a suggestion regarding the decorations. He wants us to have some.

"Nothing elaborate or stupid. Maybe just a string of lights."

What Trevor doesn't understand is that My Hate is heartfelt and true and not something to be disregarded. My Hate must be respected. It is stately and grave and very sad, like an elephant in leg irons.

"I don't think so."

"Okay," Trevor sighs. "How about a log?"

We're sitting beside the flagstone fireplace, beneath the amoebae-shaped overhead lamp, in the bliss of our pure, never-renovated fifties living room. I'm wearing a puffy dress and an apron. He's drinking a martini from an angular martini glass. Previously, I had been in the back house doing bong hits with the revolting Nickles bat child, who's happy for the company, I guess. I guess no one has ever talked to him voluntarily. I knock at the window and stand outside as we pass the bong back and forth. I think it's clear to both of us that the interior of the shack is totally encrusted with semen and could be described as such, like some kind of nouvelle cuisine entrée, monkfish, and that it would be wholly unacceptable for me to set foot inside. So I stay out in the yard, leaning against the parts of the shack that have been rinsed by rainwater. The Bat Boy and I agree that the marijuana makes the lights look more interesting.

"A log?"

"Yes."

"A log and only a log?"

"Yeah. Here's the thing. It's pagan."

Trevor shows me an article from a Christian newspaper called *Good News*. It explains that Jesus was not actually born in December, but in midsummer. The article goes on to urge Christians to stop celebrating Christmas, because it is a pagan holiday bequeathed to us by hairy Druids who worshipped trees, wine, beasts, mind-bending herbs, and the holy fertility of vaginas.

"Those pagans sound just like Hell's Angels."

"Kind of," Trevor says, with some doubt in his voice.

I dust off my apron and pick out a log from the bin of firewood beside the fireplace and carry it out the door. There are maybe a hundred pedestrians on the sidewalk in front of our house at that hour, gawking at the decorations on either side, bundled up, singing, holding cups of spiced cider, faces awash in golden light—and they all turn to look at me when I open the door. Who am I? I might be Santa! Trevor leans against the doorway pinching a martini glass like Cary Grant. I walk to the center of the lawn. I heave the log from my chest and it thuds into the center of a square of winter grass and lodges there. A log and only a log.

It looks rather festive.

———

Sometimes I wonder what the Bat Boy thinks about all this. It's hard to tell. As I open the gate between our yards and approach the shack, he bounces up and down as though I'm his favorite babysitter and says, "Dude, guess what? Guess what? I watched the *Twilight Zone* marathon today!" He's pudgy, with close-set eyes sunk deeply into his head. His face is greasy, and sometimes a hair protrudes from his nose. Weirdly, the Bat Boy has a deep, baritone voice, which gives him an air of maturity undercut by his tendency to mouth-breathe, to chuckle vacantly, to rehash eighties slang. He often shields his eyes with his hands while we're talking, as though I am a blinding light. I don't mind, as he's so nauseating that I can barely bring myself to look at him full in the face, anyway.

"Any good?"

"Bitching," he booms.

I lean against the windowsill of the back house and accept the bong while, in the background, wafting on the breeze, floats the statement "It's a holly, jolly Christmas." The bong is made of blue plastic, and the little bowl is packed with pungent sinsemillan. The Bat Boy gets it from Fat Man, who comes by once a week, a lifetime supply of adipose rolling around beneath his T-shirt—one of his few other visitors.

The Bat Boy gestures toward the bong and says, "It's like it sucks your brain out, puts it in a Cuisinart, then pours it back in your skull all smooth."

Indeed, he is correct. I look out over the Nickles backyard and feel the smooth-brain beauty of night in the desert: crisp but not cold, the moon above like a spotlit Chihuahua, the Christmas lights blinking in the neighborhood beyond, so unreal. So totally fake, the cheer and goodwill and such. The Bat Boy starts his strange, guttural chuckle. Sometimes he seems just slightly off in his manner, as though he'd spent a few seminal years in another country—maybe France. Then he talks about going to the salad bar with his mother and filling his plate with raisins and I realize that there's something deeply wrong with him. I'm worried for the Bat Boy. He's thirty-five and has never done his own laundry. My God, who wouldn't be worried for the Bat Boy? He's clearly in the throes of something universal and corrupt. He smells sour. He doesn't floss. He looks at me with his sunken eyes. I'm probably the only woman who has ever spoken to him more than once, aside from his mother. He knocks the bowl against the side of the shack and the ashes sprinkle out. I have a question for him.

"You know that song 'Jingle Bells'?"

The Bat Boy nods.

"What kind of weird grammatical thing is going on with that 'jingle'? What is it? Is it an imperative verb? An adjective? The horse's *name*?"

The Bat Boy stares at me blankly, then says, "It's the bells." He chuckles and adds, "They jingle."

That is what the Bat Boy thinks of all this.

Later his mother tells me that he can play "Flight of the Bumblebee" on the piano flawlessly. But nothing else. Not even "Chopsticks."

Elsa comes over and talks and talks but doesn't listen, as is the way with Elsa. She's an artist with willowy arms, neck, and legs and a big fat ass that I would never dream of mentioning if I liked her better. She paints transgressive portraits of dead animals (as, curiously, have nearly all the artists I've ever known). Trevor finds her sort of relaxing. "Because you never need to worry about making conversation when Elsa is around."

"I know people who would kill for this audience," she says.

"Audience?"

"These crowds outside. These hordes of people. Where can you find a gathering like that? An audience that possesses the gaze, that sees, yet without anticipating art or even beauty."

"They're just here to look at our log." Trevor is sipping a cocktail called a Gibson, which is a martini containing something that isn't an olive—possibly a cotton ball.

Elsa continues on as though no one else had spoken. "Yet they come to behold, to witness a visual experience. Something transcendent, beyond the seasonal. Beyond the Santa or the Rudolph or the tripartite Snow Man."

"I don't really think of it as transcendent. More like torture."

Elsa fixes me with her chilly stare. "Right. Well, you can whine about it, or you can use it as inspiration to make something better." She bites a nail. "You should do something with this. You should make a statement."

"A statement?"

"Exactly. Like art. Like some really motherfucking intense art." Elsa walks to the window and flings open the curtains. She gestures toward the bedazzled neighborhood overrun with children and carolers and grandparents and horsies. They all look back in at us through the window. "What is this, if not a vernacular form of installation art?"

"Christmas decorations?" I venture.

Elsa looks at me with disdain, as is the way with Elsa. "Get out of your head," she advises. "Get out of your head and into the world."

I'm mellowing out with Steely Dan's "Gaucho," trying to block out the caroling, when my mother calls. My mother— always helpful, always striving. She's the last of that generation of women who were not expected to have jobs or even hobbies. Therefore, she's been forced to hurl herself into the business of others, endlessly, day and night, just to keep herself busy, the poor thing. She's become fascinated by the holiday occupation of our neighborhood.

"Wouldn't it be terrific if you had kids of your own," she says. "They'd be so excited!"

"I'm sure they'd be apoplectic. But wouldn't you want them to be more Jewish?"

"Of course, but I'm thinking about the lights. Lights don't have religion. They're universal."

"They twinkle." I start to laugh, because I'm stoned. Which is basically the only time that I get along with my mother.

She starts to laugh too. "They do! We had beautiful lights on the house on Lawndale Avenue when I was a girl."

"What?" I stop laughing. "What?"

"And angels. Fabulous, golden angels."

"What did you say?"

"I said 'angels.' Don't worry, they were nondenominational. There are plenty of angels in the Old Testament."

"You never told me this."

To honor our Jewish heritage, and according to my parents' wishes, my own girlhood was spent without lights, trees, stockings, Santa, eggnog, or goodwill of any kind. My parents generally spent Christmas day doing yard work while my brother and I watched undesirable Christmas specials on TV. An effort was made to substitute Hanukkah, but it drifted around on the calendar from year to year in a way that made it hard to take seriously.

"I didn't tell you? That's funny. I must have mentioned the tree?"

"What are you saying? That you had a Christmas tree?"

"Oh, well. Not every year."

"You had a tree?"

"It's not important. It just occurred to me that Grandma might still have the angels in her garage. Maybe we could send them to you. You could put them on the lawn."

"I don't want them."

"I'll just poke around."

"Did you hear me just say I don't want them?"

"Well, that's fine. That's not a problem. The last thing I want to do is go digging through bins of my mother's garbage."

———

The nondenominational angels arrive in a giant box two days later, overnighted. For some reason, perhaps because Trevor is busy working, I decide to take one over to show to the Bat Child. It's evening. The lights are just twinkling on, and the police barricades that keep out nonlocal traffic (except for horse-drawn hay carts) are just being set up. Christmas hangs in the air like a fetid odor. I have a terrible feeling in my stomach, true dread, as though I will always be exiled. I will be stuck in the most horrible place imaginable, a seventies fern bar, while everyone else is happy and full of cheer. Everyone else is gathered in front of the fire, decorating a tree, singing about love, while I sit alone on a dirty wooden bench with my feet scraping the orange shag carpet, droning *Christ their lord.*

The Bat Boy slides open the window and hands me the bong. He has the waxy look of the unwashed, and a fold of belly hangs out from under his shirt. I accept the bong and press my mouth to the plastic tube. It only takes a moment to realize that what we are smoking this evening is some truly choice marijuana, deeply spectacular. I look in the bowl. Within is a half-burned bud, sparkling with resin. The Fat Man has outdone himself. Almost immediately upon exhaling I possess a clarity that allows me to see the nature of things in their truest, deepest aspect.

"Good weed."

The Bat Boy nods sagely. "Most definitely. Excellent. Fat Man called it 'Truth Teller.'"

I nod. Yes, truth. It's everywhere.

"I've been smoking it all day." He looks into the middle distance and says, "Now I understand."

I giggle.

"Beam me up," the Bat Boy says, and I giggle harder. I feel something under my arm and look down to see the angel. I hold it up to show the Bat Boy. The angel has a sweet, porcelain face, like a genderless doll. It's as big as a three-year-old. He/she is dressed in golden robes that end just above a pair of little black slippers. The Bat Boy and I stare at the angel for a while. I can see the deepest, truest aspect of things, and what I see is this: the angel is adorable.

The Bat Boy shrinks back into his shack and, in his sonorous voice so full of wisdom and stupidity, says, "Holy shit. That thing is evil. Get it away from me."

Then he withdraws into the shack and snaps the window shut.

One advantage—the only advantage—to the Occupation is that it provides an excess of light, people, and police protection, which allows me to walk around my own neighborhood alone at night. Therefore, I am feeling very independent and stoned as I amble around later that evening, looking at the Santas dragging their bellies on the rooftops, the reindeer pawing the air, the lampposts striped like candy canes. I go all the way to Gavin Road, and it's getting so cold on the way back that I have to put my hood up. The streets are half-empty but the lights are still going full force, twinkling like demons. Some people really have gone all-out. One family has filled its front yard with polyester batting, to give us desert-dwellers the feeling of snow. Little soft-sculpture children throw "snowballs" at a floppy soft-sculpture man. Other homeowners have barely tried or tried strangely and failed, like the house decorated entirely in blue lights, glowing like a gigantic bottle of Windex.

When I'm nearly home I notice that someone is following me, darting behind me from tree to tree like a secret agent. Who is it? Why, it's the Bat Boy! Why is he following me? Because no other girl has talked to him in twenty years, so of course he's madly in love with me.

I guess I forgot to mention that.

———

Because nature abhors a vacuum, we put the angels on the front lawn, halfheartedly, propped beside the log. They are not properly lit. They are not staked to the earth and could be stolen. We are not trying very hard, due to My Hate, and I feel stupid and hypocritical to be trying at all. But Trevor has been bitten by the spirit of the season and thinks the angels are cute, so who am I to extinguish his joy and cheer and tell him not to drink so much? Why shouldn't he drink gallons and gallons of martinis? God knows, I'm getting stoned often enough with the Bat Child, who's probably imagining me posed in revolting sexual tableaux involving elves even as I stumble back into our swank, fifties living room with a slack jaw and bloodshot eyes, smelling like bong water. At this, Trevor fails to blink an eye. He has never asked where I go every night when I slip out the sliding glass door and disappear for thirty or forty minutes. I don't think he's even noticed.

But he does notice this: several days after we put the angels in the yard, we come home from an outing to find that someone has been tampering with our angels. Someone has been *fucking* with them, more accurately. There are four angels. We find that two of them have been buried head-down in the yard so that their little legs are waving immodestly in the air. The other two are splayed, cruciform, across a couple of prickly pear cacti, their garments rent by thorns. Oh my. It looks quite uncomfortable. But that's not all! Someone has been very busy. Written largely across the lawn, in tiny white lights held down by wires, is the word *Evil*. An extension cord snakes over to an outdoor outlet on the side of the Nickles house.

"Wow," says Trevor. "Wow. When did you do this?"

"I didn't."

Trevor follows me into the house saying, "I don't get you," and, "Did you do that to piss me off?" and, "That's actually psychotic," while I keep repeating that I didn't do it. But Trevor will not believe me until I finally break down and explain about the Bat Boy and the bong and the semen-encrusted shed and the evenings we've spent together, passing crackers smeared with orange paste back and forth through the sliding window, passing the blue bong back and forth, talking, giggling, until Trevor starts to get a wounded look around the eyes. Then finally he does understand, and goes into his office and says he doesn't want to talk to me right now.

"Hey," I say through the door. "Hey, why don't you come out for a minute. Do the Chinese restaurant waiter! Do the angry Belgian pastry chef!"

I wait. Nothing.

I guess Trevor is not going to do any funny voices for me today.

———

That night I sit in the splendor of our perfect fifties living room, in the dark, listening to the crowd shuffle by outside our picture window. Sometimes I hear nothing and sometimes I hear a kind of angry murmuring, the kind that might be made by a group of men in Klan outfits. For the moment I have switched to martinis. I imagine the gaze of the public falling upon our angels with buried heads. Our angels impaled on prickly pear. Maybe this is educational: when bad things happen to good angels. Every now and then I peek out the window. The log is still there! Valiant little guy. People are throwing trash at our display to express their displeasure. A couple of people ring our doorbell, hoping to express their displeasure in person.

I'm enjoying my martini. I can understand what Trevor sees in them. It's like smoking pot, but with more hostility and extra trips to the bathroom.

———

The next morning, I get up and start picking trash out of our front yard, feeling a trifle ill. The neighborhood looks truly desperate in the light of day, with everyone's decorations turned off and washed-out in the flat desert light, the road littered with piles of horse shit bisected by tire tracks. There is nothing like Christmas in Arizona, azure skies and seventy-two degrees, to make the world look fraudulent. Someone has put a Big Gulp cup over the foot of one of the angels. It smells somewhat uriney, and I'm wondering if someone actually *peed* on one of the angels when a feeling comes upon me, a little engine of prissiness. I decide what I'm going to do. I'm going to tell. So I march next door and ring the bell.

Cindy answers wearing a ruffled green and red bathrobe. She already has her eye makeup on, and she's talking on the phone. She makes me wait for a while and then rolls her eyes and tells me she's on hold—can I be quick?

I tell her that I think she should know her son has made an unholy diorama depicting the graphic torture of angels on our lawn.

She gives me a level gaze. "Floyd didn't do that. Floyd likes to stay in the back house."

"Yeah, but the thing is, he did."

She presses her lips together. "Floyd likes to stay in the back house. Jim! Jim?"

Jim's voice floats through the door. "What?"

"Honey, where does Floyd like to stay?"

He echoes her singsong tone: "Floyd likes to stay in the back house."

She looks at me through wide, mascara-framed eyes. "See?" And then she closes the door.

———

That night a police cruiser stops in front of our house and sits there with its lights flashing against our window for a while and then drives off. More trash is thrown. The doorbell rings twice. I ignore all this and spend the hours of the Occupation watching a movie called *Endless Summer 2*, about a pair of suntanned boys who roam the planet surfing beautiful, blue waves. Every now and then I get up and listen at the door to Trevor's office. He's in there, tap-tapping on his computer.

Of course, the obvious thing to do is to remove the angels. Why not? Really. I've already tried twice. But each time, I end up just standing on the lawn, staring at them, just staring like a zombie. I cannot do it. I just can't. We had good times together, the Bat Boy and I, smoking out, gazing off at his old tetherball pole with the withered globe at the end, his mother's voice whining across the yard from the big house. There is no sanctuary like the sanctuary of outsiders; there is no fellowship like the fellowship of the scorned. Deep inside we all have a Bat Boy, echolocating inside an empty cave, forever shunned, hated, misunderstood, smelly, flinging our ardor unsuitably, desperately, making strange things in the hope of attracting love. Who am I to say this is wrong?

Furthermore, we're in agreement. Christmas is evil.

Days pass. Somewhere, elsewhere, someone is opening the little doors of an Advent calendar. Trevor will not move the display and I will not move the display and it's obviously bothering him. I infer this when Trevor stops talking to me altogether.

"Hey!" I say as he passes me in the hallway, "who's the slowest mouse in the whole world?" But he doesn't even look tempted to break down and do the voice of Slowpoke Rodriguez, the stereotypical Warner Brothers mouse who I generally nix as too offensive, though Trevor does his accent so well.

I have forsaken the Bat Boy and his sticky weed for several days because I am a person of conscience and morals and his behavior has weirded me out. But Trevor won't talk to me, and our friends are off doing Christmas things that don't involve us, and no one likes me anyway, I've decided. I'm ill-tempered and bitter. Like Socrates, I cannot stop disabusing people of various joyously held notions and beliefs. Who wants to indulge my scowling? Nobody. Of course, people are warm and full of spirit at this time of year, but I am lonely, lonely—if only I had a wonderful little dog to look at me with adoring eyes, while I work alone in my drafty room and Trevor works next door, alone in his drafty room—I think about this until, finally, I feel so forlorn and sad that I decide to go back.

The light is on in the Bat Boy's shed but he's nowhere in sight. Usually he's waiting for me, leaning against the sliding window as if he's ready to take my order. I pad across the grass and look inside. Bat Boy is lying on his back on his cot beside a reading lamp. One hand is at his side, touching the bong. His face is relaxed. What is he doing? He's staring at the ceiling. I tap the glass.

In one movement, the Bat Boy swings his feet to the floor and starts loading up the bong. He leans over, chuckling softly, and slides the window open.

"I thought you weren't coming back."

"No, I'm here."

"Dude," he says, with sadness, "I thought you weren't coming back."

"Floyd."

"You're going to love this herb."

"Floyd."

He chuckles. "That's my name, don't wear it out."

"Okay, I just have to ask you. Did you do that to our angels? Did you, uh, *reconfigure* them?"

"Yeah, yeah. Wicked, isn't it?"

"Sort of. Some people don't like it though."

"They're just bugging."

"Yeah. They are. They're bugging on our doorstep."

"My mom and dad are totally bugging. They don't like it AT ALL." He chuckles and hands me the bong.

I take a hit of the sweet, sticky smoke. "Really? It's better than their lame-assed Wise Men."

"You think?"

"My God. A thousand times better."

The Bat Boy's hand creeps across the windowsill until it rests on top of my own. He squeezes. I'm pretty certain he's been picking his nose with those fingers. But for some reason, I squeeze back.

———

Elsa starts hanging around, taking photographs. At first she's half-angry, half-excited that we've taken her advice and created some really motherfucking intense artwork in the yard.

"I can't believe it," she keeps saying, and also: "I hope you're telling people this was my idea. I want full credit." Elsa on this particular afternoon is wearing a parka splattered with paint and a pair of shorts she found in the garbage—she is sure to tell us this, because she wants us to know that she thinks buying clothing is repulsively bourgeois. "This is great," she keeps repeating, snapping away with her camera, "this is anti-everything. Anti-religion, anti-neighborhood, anti-beauty. I can't believe your neighbors haven't lynched you."

If I could wedge in a word, I would wedge in the word *yet*.

Eventually Elsa stops talking long enough for me to explain that in truth, we didn't make the motherfucking intense angel thing. Trevor nods. He's not talking to me, but he'll talk to Elsa.

"We didn't make it. We just leave it there," he says. "We want full credit for that."

"It was our neighbor," I chime in. "Our autistic, pot-smoking, dysfunctional neighbor whose parents keep him in a little shack and pretend he doesn't exist."

"Oh my God," says Elsa, and stands there for a second, momentarily struck dumb. "That is so unbelievably cool."

———

Another day passes, another little door opens, and presto, it's Christmas Eve. What makes stupid things happen? Every schoolchild knows the answer to this: drugs mixed with alcohol. Even as I resume smoking pot, I keep up with my martinis, until finally all the lines get a little blurrier. All the elves get a little sillier. Okay, fine: I'll say it. On Christmas Eve, the Bat Boy and I get stoned and make out. He grabs my hand and looks at me with adoring eyes, then, while chuckling, he leans toward me until his lips are pressed against mine. I stand on the outside of the shack. He stays on the inside. We pull apart. He looks at me with his sunken eyes and says, "Dude." After a while I decide I'm cold and join him on the inside. I don't know what I'm thinking. I guess I want something new on a crisp, winter night: two people united in hate for the holidays. I think it could make the world shine and/or twinkle. I can't say I recommend it. Kissing the Bat Boy is like mouthing something that has been stored in a trunk for a very long time. Still, I feel assured that no one had been there before me, and no one will be there after, that for him at least, this is something very special. A sackful of joy.

Before I go, he says, "Don't leave."

"I have to."

"Let me come with you."

"Absolutely not." I climb back out the window and into the blurriness of his yard.

What can I say? There is no sanctuary like the sanctuary of oddballs taking refuge in one another. There is no loyalty like the loyalty of the scorned.

Two days later, the shack is empty. The bong is nowhere in sight. It's empty the day after, and the day after that. I corner Cindy in the driveway, who cheerfully tells me that Floyd the Bat Child has finally moved out. Out! He's moved in with his girlfriend, Elsa Hammer, a lovely girl and a fantastic artist. Did I know her?

"I thought Floyd liked to stay in the back house."

"Let me tell you a little secret." Cindy leans closer until I'm swimming in her perfume. "Floyd hated the shack. He always hated the shack. But we couldn't have him in the house. Not all day long."

"I thought he liked it. I thought he wanted his privacy."

"Are you crazy? He detested it out there."

"No."

"Yes. He wanted to be in the big house with us," Cindy touches a smug finger to the corner of her mouth, "but he was getting too old. We thought he should be independent."

"I don't believe you. It was his shack. He loved it."

"Floyd," says Cindy, "always hated that shack." And then, singing out: "Jim, what did Floyd hate?"

Jim's voice floats out of the big house: "The shack."

———

Eventually, Trevor starts talking to me again. Even after Christmas is over, I keep listening to my CD of the Steve Miller Band and Trevor makes up new words to the chorus: "I'm a joker / I'm a smoker / I'm a real estate broker." He mixes up a few martinis and we drink them together and then I do interpretive dances on the flagstone patio while he watches for a while, then goes inside to finish up some work. I dig the angels out of the yard and put them in the trash. Christmas is finally over, New Year's is past, Valentine's Day, Easter. The days get longer and hotter. In the afternoons, I put on my suit and float around in the pool, looking up at the clouds, feeling pissed off and betrayed while telling myself I shouldn't. What's the big deal? All Floyd did was use art to get chicks, as millions of painters and poets and guitar-playing boys have before him. Isn't that why people make things in the first place? To say all the things that have such power but sound so tame when we say them flat out: that we want love, that we're lonely, that we hate the shack, that we've always hated the shack, that we're afraid we're in the process of wasting our lives.

As for me, I've decided that I do not hate the shack, that I shall not conduct a life spent hating the shack. Yuletide Village is where we live. We picked this god-awful place, and a series of events will be happening here every December. Why can't our part of it be pagan? What did Elsa say— if you don't like something, you can complain about it, or you can make something better yourself? Fine. We can venerate our own gods. In our yard there will be no cheer, no light, no hope, no merriness. But I've decided there will be drunkenness, wild beasts, potent herbs, vaginas, and log after log after log.

We are designing the display now.

BLACKOUT

The *worst night of my life?* A couple of years ago we were all down in Baja for spring break and a bunch of guys were slipping roofies into girls' drinks. I don't know where they got them since all the farmacias had hand-lettered signs warning NO ROOFIES!!! but I suppose some joker must have had a stash left over from a previous year of merrymaking. We were in Tequila Rudolph's and all these girls were just so fucked up, beyond drunk, and believe me, some of those chicks can drink like longshoremen. They were throwing up or passing out, stumbling around on rubbery legs—much like winos but with blonde streaks and little tank tops and phones tucked into their waistbands. Some friends of mine I now don't like were dancing on the furniture and taking off their shirts, so naturally all the guys were yelling, "*Show us your tits!*" Those girls would have done it anyway, even without the knockout pills. (Therize, later: "I love spring break!!!") Sure, we all know the concept of the date-rape drug is to slip a girl a roofie and then take her back to your hotel, where she conveniently passes out in your room, bypassing the need for good looks, chitchat, or hygiene. But these guys were too lame to actually arrange the date part. They were just dumping drugs into girls' drinks, hoping they could maneuver them home later. Bad planning had saved the day, since the girls were too wasted to reliably walk. As I heard it, almost everybody was still in the bar in the morning, sleeping under the tables.

Anyway, this Kappa named Sandra was there and I just always hated her guts, because she was so skinny with big breasts and could eat whatever she wanted without gaining, bloating, or sticking her finger down her throat. In fact, she had no neurotic body issues as far as I could tell—why did the Kappas even let her pledge? Masochism? I had a couple of classes with her and she was smart, too, but a real bitch who stole other girls' boyfriends and slept with professors to get straight As for no work, or so my friends said. Our houses were next door to each other, so sometimes at the gym she'd come up to me and say hello. She wore a little pair of workout shorts that had the word *perfect* printed in big letters on the ass. Occasionally we'd ride the stationary bikes together. Usually we'd talk about parties or how many turns to turn down the waist of our shorts so our abs showed (her abs), but one time she told me a little story about herself.

Apparently, she'd been a great trick rider when she was a kid. Every day after school she'd take her BMX out and practice in the driveway. Sandra could do a wheelie while twirling the front tire all the way around (she explained as we labored on the Lifecycles with our ponytails swinging back and forth); she could do a handstand on the seat while the bike rolled down a hill. None of the neighborhood boys could touch her in skill or daring, and they broke bones trying. I could see the proud little girl in her face as she described how she blew them away, though she also mentioned something about having to ride alone since the boys got mad, and slashed her tires with jack knives, and spread rumors at school about how she was a major slut, until after a while she became an untouchable at the junior high level.

"I had no friends," Sandra said, and took a slug off her water bottle. "Zero. It was really awful. Finally I left the bike under our station wagon and my mom backed over it, and after that got around, everyone at school liked me again!"

And everyone had liked her ever since!!!

I was not dosed that night at Tequila Rudolph's, because I was reading this cool book in Great Western Authors about a defiant little clerk, so when a guy shoved a glass at me and said, "You should just fucking *quaff* this apple schnapps," I simply replied, "I prefer not to."

From then on, events degenerated. My friends were up on a table removing their bras; guys were dancing around with bras on their heads. Everyone was yelling "woo!" What I really wanted was a tequila shot, so I slid up to the bar where the bartender was cringing in the corner. That's where I found Sandra, swaying with her eyes closed, as though listening to a jazz standard. I said, "Hi, Sandra," and nothing happened. She was far away, in her own world, drooling a little. I should add that I didn't exactly know about the roofies yet, though I had a sense that something had already gone wrong with the night, like these were the early scenes of a horror movie—the revelry before the kill. But how could I have known? The big thing during spring break was to drink a lot, anyway. Sandra was drooling and I was smiling because beside her stood this guy Hans, a Gamma on whom I had the most painful crush—a knife to my ovaries. I could feel it twist when I looked at him. He had one of those big, muscled chests, hairless, bronzed, a beautiful face, a boy as golden as the Mexican sunset. He drove a Beemer.

At that point, Hans was my future. I could totally see myself marrying him. Sure, I wanted a career, but I also wanted kids and I could imagine myself scurrying between kindergarten and Pilates class the day before Hans and I hosted a dinner party. Who needs a real job? I would have all sorts of duties. Taking the SUV into the shop. Pleasing Hans in our marital bed. But he didn't look at girls like me—slightly hog-faced, in size 12 pants, someone who tried too hard and smiled too much. He was more likely to register a gazelle like Sandra. I slipped my hand through her arm.

"Are you feeling okay?"

Sandra didn't open her eyes. She mumbled, "Ma zing," which I took to mean, "amazing."

Hans leaned across her and said, "Hi, Kylie."

"Hi!" He knew my name?

"So, I think she's really wasted." He nodded at Sandra.

"I know!"

"I think she could use a hand. Wanna help me get her out of here?" He smiled.

He was so helpful! "Okay!"

I took an arm. Hans took the other. A strobe light was freezing the chaos in Tequila Rudolph's into a stream of sleazy tableaux: half-naked girls vomiting! Couples leg-wrestling on tables! It was like the fall of Rome, total decadence and an utter lack of self-reflection. I didn't want to leave. But there was Hans, smiling at me and trying to keep Sandra from falling over.

We maneuvered her out the door into the old town, the cobbled streets half paved-over, the whitewashed buildings reflecting the moonlight. She stumbled and rolled her tongue and said, "Later, later, later" (or waiter, waiter, waiter?). I had to lean in and prop her against my shoulder. She was heavy—though more floppy than weighty.

"Whoa," Hans exclaimed, "she's pretty sauced, isn't she?"

"Yeah, totally!" This was nice. We were conversing. We were getting to know each other. "So, where's she staying?"

"Uh, I don't know." Hans looked straight ahead. His profile was killing me. I'm sure it was obvious that I had a crush on him. Some Mexican men in a doorway were laughing, probably at me. Hans said, "Let's just take her to my place."

"Oh. Okay."

We walked for a while in silence. I think that Sandra had basically passed out. I remember her head hanging forward on her neck. My shoulders hurt from carrying her, and Hans's face had started to sweat. I was trying to convince myself that he had a great reason for this, for squiring a nearly comatose girl off to his room. I couldn't think what it could be, but I was sure he had one. Hans was one of those guys. He got what he wanted because he'd always got what he wanted—not by craft or charm but by the sheer weight of expectation. Twenty-one years of being the golden boy: mommy, daddy, teachers, coaches, hog-faced Chi Omegas.

We arrived at Hans' place, a chalet-style condo by the beach. Whomever he was sharing it with was not home. The place was tidy. There were a few piles of clothes folded on the back of the couch, beneath a giant, peeling photograph of an orange sunset.

"Let's put her where she can stretch out."

We unfolded Sandra onto a bed. Her little shortie top had ridden up, exposing those notorious abs. I sat on one side of the mattress and Hans sat on the other. The bed was covered with a gray and red Mexican blanket, scabbed with lint balls.

Hans coughed, then said, "That was a great party you guys gave for homecoming. The luau theme was really creative."

"Thanks!" His shirt was half-unbuttoned. Did he shave his chest, or did it just lack hair? "I agree. It was awesome."

"I'd never had one of those rum and pineapple drinks. What do you call them?"

"A stinger!"

"Yeah. It was good."

"I know! I had like eight."

This was a hookup, absolutely. Me and Hans, alone together, with Sandra. I noticed that his hand was resting on top of hers. I was staring at it; I kept telling myself to stop.

"So, how long have you known Sandra?"

"What?" Hans seemed to be slipping into some void, but he pulled himself out and said, "Yeah, Sandra. Since sophomore year. We've been hanging out a lot."

"That's great." I smiled. I kept smiling. Of course I knew this to be a lie. I'd been keeping tabs on Hans.

He was staring at Sandra's motionless body and breathing through his mouth. We were drunk. Why else would we even be there? I started to stare at Sandra, too. Her beauty was fascinating. There wasn't a pore visible on her nose, and even after dragging her through the Mexican streets, her hair tumbled back from her face in a wave, shiny and thick. She looked so milky and clean that I had an urge to dig my nails into her skin.

Then Hans put his hand in my hair and dragged me forward into a kiss. At first I didn't know what he was doing and I had to plant my hand on his leg to keep from falling into Sandra. We kissed for a while, sloppy and boozed, and when he pulled back for air I saw that he'd pushed Sandra's shirt up around her armpits. Not a bra in sight. I watched him caress her breasts. Maybe caress is not the word. Manipulate. They were just perfect, bigger than perfect. I wanted more tequila. I wanted this to be happening in a different way. I could handle sex the way I imagined it when I was eight, with Ken on top of Barbie, but I couldn't quite identify what was going on here.

Sandra was lying very still and her face was impassive. I got worried and checked her pulse to verify that she was alive and clocked her at about forty beats per minute. Hans scooped in and kissed me again, with way too much tongue, but I was still so floored that Hans was kissing me at all that I just went with it. He'd kiss me better when we were married and living in our Tuscan-style mansion. He'd kiss me better once I wore his diamond ring. He took my hand and put it on Sandra's other breast. We kept making out, our hands roaming over each other and Sandra, who lay there on the blanket like a big, warm doll. There was something so incredibly wrong with this that it was absolutely magnetic, compelling, and though I disliked myself for doing it, there was no way I was going to stop. Sluttiness was frowned upon in the house of Chi Omega, in particular any lesbian activity, including threesomes or whatever this was, but all bets were off during spring break. God only knew what my sisters had been up to. I heard them whispering about each other in the halls.

Even so, I was surprised when Hans pulled away from me and began to unbutton Sandra's shorts. "It's okay," he said, as though he had obtained prior permission. Sandra was so inert that I'd begun to think of her as not really being there. But as Hans went for her fly she sputtered back to life for a second, rubbing a hand across her nose and saying something: "medicine," maybe, or "impediment."

Hans reached for me again, but he didn't seem to be that into it anymore, and after a few minutes, he pulled away. He took his hands off me. He just kept looking at Sandra, fondling her body, tugging at her remaining clothes. I was losing. I was losing to Sleeping Beauty.

"Maybe we should roll her onto her side," I suggested.

"Why?" Hans's tone was hostile.

"This alcohol counselor said you're supposed to do that if people are really drunk. So they don't choke if they vomit, you know?"

Hans stared at me. The look said: *How the fuck did you get here?* He'd dropped all pretense of being interested in me; in fact, he looked like he hated me. Then he put the pretense back on, just like that, like a coat. He grinned and gave me a peck on the lips and said, "Kylie, I have an idea. I want you to play a game with me."

"Okay. What game?"

"Truth or dare."

He was pinching Sandra's nipples. She wasn't moving but I could see her pupils sweeping back and forth under her eyelids.

Hans coughed. "You go first."

"Can I not go first?"

"I'll flip you for it."

He fished a quarter out of his pocket and tossed it into the air. It landed with a slap on Sandra's stomach. I hadn't called it but when it came up tails Hans informed me that I'd lost; by then it seemed clear that I was just going along with whatever he said anyway.

"I'll take dare."

"Great," Hans cocked his head to the side. He was damn good-looking. "Okay. I dare you to go into the kitchen and bake a cake for me."

"What?"

"What *what*? That's your dare. There's a box of chocolate cake mix somewhere. We brought it with us."

Hans eyes smoldered in the middle of his honey-colored cheeks. What was he? A shark? Those eyes were very gray, very dead. Oh. Now I could see what was happening. Everything clicked into place. I was not going to be the wife of Hans. I was not going to be his girlfriend. He was not husband material, nor was he boyfriend material. He was a rapist. And I had been helping him.

Then I helped him some more by leaving the room and quietly closing the door behind me.

———

Here's the part that bothers me the most: I really did bake the cake. I went out into Hans's little orange and beige condo kitchen and turned on the oven; I found the cake mix and a dented aluminum baking pan in a dirty cabinet and with these tools whipped up a chocolate cake for Hans while he stayed in the other room with Sandra's body. I could hear something happening through the door. I tried not to think about it, or I tried to think that it didn't matter because I hated Sandra, but that didn't work very well, because I wasn't thinking of her as the perfect girl with the perfect ass anymore. Sometime during the course of the evening, she'd turned into the little girl who'd put her bike under a station wagon because she'd scared the boys so witless that they went around school saying she'd do anything with anyone.

I decided one thing, at least, while I was baking. I wasn't going to just leave her there for Hans's roommates to fuck when they got home.

After a while, Hans emerged from the bedroom. By then the cake was cooling in the pan on top of a wooden trivet. Hans cut a piece and ate it while leaning over the sink. We didn't speak. There was no point. I could hear the ocean pounding about six houses away. I was draining a mugful of tequila and not feeling terribly lucid. Hans picked up the half-empty bottle.

"Did you open this?"

"Yes."

Our eyes met.

I said, "You'll have to help me get her out."

"What?" Hans blinked. I stumbled past him into the bedroom to check Sandra. He had put all her clothes back on. What a tidy person. He'd go far in life. I poked her a few times. Nothing. At that moment I actually thought it was possible that Hans would attack *me*—he had turned from my future husband into a villain that quickly—but he was docile, almost bored. He helped me drag Sandra off the bed without comment, and he helped me load her into one of the golf carts that passed as a taxicab in that coastal town. I told the driver to take us back to Tequila Rudolph's. It was so quiet. I don't think there's anything as quiet as riding in a golf cart at night—no sound at all but the soft whine of the electric motor. When we got to the bar, the cabby helped me bring Sandra inside. We arranged her on a picnic table beside a dozen passed-out girls, a bevy of

sleeping beauties, wiped clean of thought or memory, totally blacked-out. More than anything, I wanted to lie
down and be one of them.

Before I left, Hans had said, "Thanks for the cake."

And I'd replied, "You're welcome."

Sometimes I see Sandra walking around school; she
passes by me with absolutely no expression on her face,
which is the same way I walk by Hans, who's become more
popular than ever. Boys can do whatever they want. They all
just graduate and start working for Endeavor Rental Car
anyway. They're all part of a giant boys' club that seems so
natural to them they probably don't even realize it exists.
Sandra got her hair cut short and looks even prettier, like a
model, with her big eyes and egg-shaped head. All the Kappas with their ponytails agree it takes true beauty and guts
to pull off a pixie cut, so Sandra is enjoying a newfound status. I see them clustered around her in the student center,
talking on their phones, comparing nail lengths, sisters who
are always in agreement with one another, even if what they
agree on sometimes is who to hate.

As for me, I moved out of my sorority house. I claimed to
have developed an allergy to the Chi Omega signature scent
(vanilla), but my sisters didn't buy it—they were like a pack
of dogs. They could smell the change in me even before
there was any sign I was breaking ranks, even before I
switched my major from Business and Marketing to English Lit. They forgot to give me phone messages. They

stopped inviting me to house dinners. It's to the point now where they won't even say hello when I run into them at parties. Therize looks through me as though I'm made of clear plastic and sniffs the air, saying, "Something smells rancid in here. Do you girls smell something *foul?*"

There are times when I think I should have dropped Great Western Authors at the beginning of the semester when I had a chance ("Nothing is less cute than a girl with a backpack full of books," Therize said). Then, when that guy offered me the schnapps, I wouldn't have had any foreign ideas in my head—I could have said anything. I could have said, *Why the fuck not?* I could have said, *Chug-a-lug!* I could have passed out under those benches in puddles of beer and vomit with the other Psi Epsilons and Kappa Kappa Sigmas and Chi Omegas. I could have been part of the carpet of sleeping beauties, content in the goodness of products and things, assured of my own innocence as we ridiculed each other and shopped and taxed our livers and vomited up cupcakes and groomed endlessly, until finally we married some Sigma Epsilon or God forbid a Gamma and settled down forever, never to think again.

Why the fuck not? Chug-a-lug. But I preferred not to.

MY MOTHER THE ROCK STAR

My mother the rock star calls Jennifer's mom a bourgeois whore for bringing me home from school in a minivan, and I say yeah, that whore, and toss a few more slices of bread on the floor, which is already strewn with food items my mother has ejected from the refrigerator because she can't think straight when the house is too neat. My mother says what are they going to do in that vile normal-mobile now? Zip to the mall and buy fuzzy bunny slippers?

And I say oh man, I hate that prissy Jennifer! and start picking up pieces of bread off the floor and putting them back in the bag.

My mother lights a cigarette and coughs dramatically until she's able to spit into the sink. She's wearing a night-gown made out of a slinky substance that glows independently of outside light. I think it's chain mail. My mother is famous for a lot of things, especially wearing great clothes and insulting people. She once told a Norwegian princess that her pink purse looked like a douche bag. My mother is so famous that she can say anything she wants to anybody.

My mother says she's going to pick up the phone and tell that Better Housekeeping replicant to stay the fuck away from her daughter. Her and her pasteboard Jennifer.

I say yeah, well . . . okay! But, are you sure? The thing my mother doesn't get is that Zoë Marcus and her mom have been giving me rides home from school for the last three months. It's either that or a limo, because I'm not allowed to take the bus. Not that she'd notice, unless she goes on a Mommy Binge.

My mother looks glassy, then tells me to give her the name of that Jennifer and her pathetic fucking phone number, too.

There's no arguing with this person. This person once told Mick Jagger he reminded her of a weather-beaten ventriloquist's dummy, only smaller. I give her Zoë's number.

My mother dials. She pauses for a moment, then instructs Mrs. Marcus to stay the fuck away from her daughter with your anal-cavity Voyager and your e-coli barbecues and your Hanes fucking *slacks*. She holds the phone in her fist and shouts in its general direction. My mother explains to Zoë's mom, or maybe her answering machine, that she is a domestic whore who sucks her husband's pathetic cock in exchange for a lifetime supply of copper Jell-O molds. She says she doesn't want weak women coming near her goddess of a daughter. She says her daughter is so much fucking better than that—that I'm a wild and brilliant force in the universe that cannot be dampened. That I am made of starlight

and can do whatever I please and it does not please me to
ride in a minivan.

Because I am better than that.

What do you want to do now? my mother asks brightly
after throwing the phone onto the tiles, where it breaks in
half. Her voice is hoarse from yelling but her makeup is perfect and her skin is flushed. She has a tiny waist and perfectly bleached hair that bounces down to the top of her
butt like a horse's tail. There's a free-form tattoo on her arm.
She says it's a portrait of God.

I want to go to the mall and get one of those plush toy
backpacks that looks like a teddy bear giving you a hug, then
go to Kristy's Krafts and look at crochet magazines. I want
to call my father at the ashram, where he has taken a vow of
silence, and listen to him tap on the phone. I want to eat a
cupcake and drink lemonade. It's my thirteenth birthday.

"Let's get you drunk!" says my mother. "You need a life
experience! Let's get you fucking plastered!"

"Plastered!" I reply. "Yeah! That sounds great!"

There's no stopping a Mommy Binge once it starts.

My mother slides into the Bricklin gracefully, and I
scramble under the broken door on the passenger side. We
peel off the grounds and into the famous California sun-
shine. My seat belt is off because my mother believes they
are harmful to our clothes. She's wearing the shimmery blue
gown she swears is made out of butterfly wings, even
though I'm too old to believe *that* anymore. Her curls whip

around in the wind. My mother's incredibly beautiful. She has a Polaroid camera set up in her dressing room so she can verify if her outfit is fabulous before she goes out; all the pictures are taped up in order on the wall and she looks fabulous in every one. She says not to trust mirrors, because they distort the essence of our beauty, but cameras only steal our souls, which we probably weren't using anyway.

I'm wearing a matching dress, only shorter and too small in the hips, because my mother is a busy rock star and cannot always find a moment to order me couture gowns, which could spoil me anyway, and maybe the sitter should just put me on a diet. I wish they'd just let me stay at my father's ashram for a while instead. I'm sure I'd lose weight there, since all they ever eat is brown rice and Swiss chard. My dad used to be an important manager who was on the phone every minute, but he had a spiritual epiphany and decided to move into the silent ashram. He gets to rake lines in the Zen garden whenever he wants. I love visiting days. My dad hugs me and smiles a lot, and we write messages to each other in the gravel.

When we arrive at the restaurant, my mother parks the Bricklin up on the sidewalk so you can't open the door to the building all the way, then puts the key on her tongue and shoves it down the valet's throat in a kiss. He looks sort of happy and scared at the same time. I've noticed a lot of people look that way around my mother. She laughs her famous, musical laugh and lights a cigarette before we go inside, where there's no smoking, of course, but my mother smokes everywhere anyway. She says what method of investigation does it take to discover a table in here, Sherlock? and the entire staff has a simultaneous conniption until everything is perfectly the way she wants it. They seat us at a large table on a platform in the center of the restaurant. It is a very queenly table. The white tablecloth has been switched to pink, because my mother says it brightens her complexion and makes me look older. They bring champagne and a pair of flutes, though my mother scowls and waves hers away. She's been doing that ever since she discovered that sobriety gives her a boundless zest for life, which was around the same time she ran naked down the street and the judge sentenced her to urine tests. We settle in and my mother orders elk carpaccio. Everyone is looking at us. She hands me a cigarette and tells me to smoke it.

The next thing that happens doesn't matter that much, because I'm never going to get a boy to like me anyway, but I notice Elliot Fineman sitting in a corner booth with his entire family. Elliot has the seat in front of me in English, and his back is so cute I can't stand it sometimes. All of Elliot's relatives are staring at us with their mouths open. The women are wearing navy blue dresses with padded shoulders and lacy white collars. The men are wearing little skullcaps, so I guess this gathering has something to do with Elliot's Bar Mitzvah, which I was not invited to, though he explained to the whole class in an oral report how it was an incredibly solemn and ancient ceremony that would ritually mark his ascension to manhood, or something.

While they're staring, my mother reaches for my glass and spoons some champagne onto the tip of each breast until you can see her nipples through the material. Elliot's tongue is starting to creep out of his mouth. His father's head sinks down on the table until all I can see is his shiny, Jewish hat. Elliot's father always wears suits and walks with a cane. Some kids call Elliot "Smelliot" or "Smigarette" because his father is a lawyer for a tobacco company, but I never get the chance to call him anything at all.

Mr. Fineman starts snapping his fingers. A manager scurries over to their table, and Mr. Fineman waves his arms around and jabs his finger at us while yelling. I think Mr. Fineman is one of those fathers who's used to having things exactly the way he wants, and when he doesn't get it, he yells. He screams at Coach Babcock if our team loses a soccer game. He is so far behind my mother in getting what he wants that I feel sort of sorry for him. When my mother orders people around, they like it. It's exciting. If my mother bothered to yell at Coach Babcock, I'm sure we'd win the championship.

My mother has been ignoring everything, but finally she looks over at Mr. Fineman yelling and pointing and says stop fucking staring at my beautiful daughter, you revolting pervert. Then she stands up, takes the bottle of champagne, and pours it down the front of her dress with boundless zest. Right away it all goes see-through and you can't help but notice that she isn't wearing any panties. She says if you must violate something with your eyes, little man, spare the child and violate me instead.

Mr. Fineman sits there with his face turning redder and redder. I'm worried, because he looks like just the kind of person who would be having a heart attack if he were a character on TV. Finally he can't stand it and jumps to his feet. He makes a lunge in our direction, waving his cane. He has to steady himself on a chair back. If by any chance there were diners who weren't staring at us before, they're staring at us now.

Meanwhile, Elliot gets up and stands with his hands in his suit pockets like nothing is happening, like his dad is just signing the check or something and Elliot is hanging out in the background, feeling mellow. His eyes catch mine for a second, and it's like he sees me, really *sees* me for the first time—and in this deeply personal moment we share, he sends out through his eyes two pure beams of distilled hate.

This isn't really all that bad. No one is ever going to want to marry me anyway, no matter how many periods of study hall I spend voodoo-writing Elliot's name combined with mine: *Yoko Fineman, Yoko Fineman.* It's not as bad as the time I invited Liza Bederman over after school, and when we walked into my house, we found my mother standing in her panties over a naked groupie. The groupie was chained to the coffee table, and my mother was spraying squiggles of Cheez Whiz into his pubic hair. She'd sprayed it all over his head, too, and his eyebrows and armpits. Liza turned to me and said um, can I use your phone? I said okay, and she called her mom and told her to come pick her up. She wouldn't even wait inside. She sat on the blacktop outside the gate, ignoring me.

Later I was crying and my mother said yeah but honey, you have to admit it was a pretty cool idea to spray Cheez Whiz all over that goofy guy. It was too bad that snotty little Jennifer went home, she said, because later she was going to put a black light on him to see if the Cheez Whiz glowed in the dark, and you have to admit us girls might think that was pretty neat.

The manager begins to maneuver Mr. Fineman toward the door. He's not exactly kicking him out, but you can tell he thinks the world would be a happier place if Mr. Fineman just left his restaurant. The ladies in the party have already stormed off anyway. Elliot is the last to slink through the door. With his face all pink, in his Bar Mitzvah suit with his curly hair springing out around his skullcap, he looks even cuter than he normally does.

My mother is triumphant and tells the waiter she wants to buy champagne for everyone. In a few minutes the restaurant is full of popping corks. My mother insists on a big glassful for me, then stands to address the room. Her butterfly dress has almost dried. Her hair cascades down her back in a lush wave. She looks like a mermaid. I can tell everyone loves her, because she's breathtaking and famous and she's bought them expensive champagne they would probably never drink otherwise, even though this is a glamorous place my mother swears is secretly owned by Marlon Brando.

I just want to say, my mother says to the room, that I gave birth to this little bud thirteen years ago, and hasn't she bloomed into a fucking incredible flower? My mother tells me to stand up, and since there's no arguing with her, I stand under the scrutiny of all the patrons. I can feel every-one looking at me and thinking, too bad she's not like her mother. The poor chubby girl, they're thinking, she probably can't sing and obviously can't dance and everyone knows that famous people's kids are the most screwed-up of any-body who isn't poor. At least Elliot isn't here thinking, there's that weird girl who always crochets doilies in the back of class—even though he probably thinks I'm knitting.

My mother says, I gave birth to her thirteen years ago and I still remember the drugs they gave me at the hospital, they were so fucking great. How about a roar of applause for my angel?

Everyone starts clapping so I bow and then turn it into a sitting-back-down, but my mother is in general unstoppable so she stands there beaming for a while, letting everyone look at her, and they all seem pretty giddy what with their champagne occasion and getting to tell everyone how they gazed upon my celebrated and ravishing mother. My mother says hey where's Brando, the fat slob? and a waiter comes over and whispers in her ear, and my mother says no, no—loudly, to the room—I just wanted to sit on his lap, which is probably one of her rare attempts to be diplomatic and so no one has any idea what she's talking about.

Finally she sits and starts to nibble her elk. I transfer most of the champagne to my water glass by holding it in my mouth then dribbling it out when my mother isn't look-ing. The waiter periodically whisks away the full cham-pagne-and-spit glass and replaces it with a fresh, empty one, while pouring bubbly at the other end of the cycle. I ask him for a cupcake and he says oh sweetie I'll bring two, in this way that's nice but also really sorry for me.

Then everyone stops by our table to ask for an autograph and to tell my mother how great she is. They tell her how much more beautiful she is in person, how that gorgeous song of hers was playing when this one guy met his wife, how seeing her love herself so fiercely without apology has helped them to love themselves better. An elegant grandmother comes over to say how dedicated her son is to my mother's poster, moving it from bedroom to dorm room to office wall over the years, and won't she sign this scrap of paper, because it will be the most meaningful memento in his entire life. In these streams of admirers, no one ever notices me, unless it's to get more attention from my mother, then they usually say what a beautiful girl, or they say my, Yoko, aren't you lucky to be your mother's daughter! I smile and don't mention how I only get to see her about once a month, and during that one day I'm miserable. Even worse, for the rest of the time I'm incredibly restless and bored, pining for the day when I can again be miserable in her presence.

The waiter returns with cupcakes with candles. My mother waves the fans back so she can make a toast. To the horrors of adolescence! she says, thank God I don't have to go through that shit again!

Everyone crowds around and begs her to sing "Happy Birthday." She refuses halfheartedly for a minute before she parts her lips and begins to belt it out. I read one magazine article that said my mother's low, grainy voice was like a partially dissolved sugar solution leaking from the radio, but for me it will always be the voice that sang me lullabies. She's just getting going when the door bursts open. A restaurant full of heads swivel around to see Mr. Fineman charging back in with his cane swinging in front of him. He's flanked by a pair of policemen with their nightsticks drawn. The policemen look very serious and their walkie-talkies buzz officially as they stomp through the room as if they don't care about Marlon Brando or how much he weighs or his fancy establishment. But when their eyes hit my mother, candlelit and just breaking into the second "to you," they melt. Instantly, they become tail-wagging puppies.

My mother has to stop singing, though, because Mr. Fineman is yelling again. That's her! he yells. That's the harpy who terrorized my family! He points at us with his cane. I guess he likes doing that, but it makes him look like a jerk. He's brought Elliot with him, and it's pretty obvious Elliot wants to sink into the floor and disappear. I sort of want to sink through the floor with him. We could live together underground and raise prairie dogs as pets. But part of me also wants to stay and see my mother crush Mr. Fineman.

That woman! Mr. Fineman waves the cane at my mother—she exposed her body in front of a male minor! That violates the law and all standards of common decency!

My mother directs her gaze to Mr. Fineman, and her eyes turn into slits. She takes a deep breath. It's as if someone rolled a grenade under our table: everyone steps back. I am not common! my mother says, slamming her hand on the table so hard the silverware jumps. She leaps to her feet, balancing expertly on her high heels, and pulls me up beside her. We stand there, looking down from our platform on Mr. Fineman and poor Elliot. I guess that just isn't high enough, because then my mother climbs on top of the table and hauls me up by the elbow to stand beside her. Looking down on Elliot like that, I can't help but think how he's one of five or six kids at school who doesn't call me Yuck-O.

I exposed nothing! my mother declares. She kicks a few plates onto the floor. It's your lecherous and degraded mind that's been exposed tonight, here in front of my darling daughter, and if you're so concerned about your delicate canary of a Billy, why didn't you have the little dumpling wait in the car? Yes! *That* is what a good parent would do, you old fruit licker!

She flicks her cigarette into a snifter of brandy on the table below. It bursts into flame.

My mother starts to glow with her queen-of-triumph glow while the policemen smirk and stand back, shaking their heads with sheer amazement at their incredible luck, to be witnessing the feisty, tabletop antics of my legendary mother.

Mr. Fineman looks from my mother to the policemen. Can you believe this nutty dame? he says. Can you believe this walking menace? He squints at the police, who are chuckling. Hey, he says, hey buddy. Aren't you going to arrest her?

What a fabulous idea, says my mother. I want to go to jail. I want to be handcuffed. She hops down from the table and prances over to a policeman. He has one of those beach-ball guts and my mother starts bouncing up against it and giving him a smoky look. He drops his keys. Of course everyone in the whole restaurant is crowding around watching and blushing, thinking bad girls will be bad girls, all except for Mr. Fineman. He must be the only person in America who doesn't know who my mother is.

Then my mother's brow shifts into an even more mischievous slant and she says maybe you'd like to be handcuffed, too. I know you old farts, you fossilized cane-brandishers, you can't get off unless you're tied to a crucifix and smeared with tapioca with a Malibu Barbie stuffed up your butt!

Lady, Mr. Fineman announces, you've gone too far.

You've gone too far. This is a phrase I've heard forever—you've gone too far this time, insulting the Princess of Wales! You've gone too far, canceling a tour of Japan and putting a thousand people out of work so that you can fly to Antarctica and eat a piece of mastodon meat from a carcass they mined from the permafrost! I've started to think of Too Far as a place you could actually visit, like Catalina Island, only cloudy, and overrun with carnivorous dinosaurs. The funny thing about Too Far is that whenever we start to approach it, it creeps back into the haze, so that no matter how many people warn us, we can never actually reach that awful place.

The cops keep smiling and laughing and taking mental pictures of this glamorous scene. My mother jokes with them and scrawls on their ticket pads. My mother always says famous people aren't above the law, they're just punished through autographs instead of jail time. I wonder if there's any illegal activity here, one of the policemen asks, and starts to swagger toward Mr. Fineman with his hand-cuffs out, as if he's going to take my mother's suggestion and make the guy some sort of jailhouse slave. Elliot slinks around in the background, blushing. Mr. Fineman grabs his head in exasperation. A shocked look pops on to his face when he discovers he's still wearing his satin cap. He snatches it off and shoves it in his pocket. Elliot said that the cap was a symbol to remind Jewish men that God is always above them, so I guess Mr. Fineman has either decided he isn't a Jewish man or that God isn't in Brando's restaurant anymore.

I'm still standing on the table, in my too-tight dress, but no one is paying any attention to me. Everyone is crowding around my mother, who has obviously forgotten all about singing "Happy Birthday." No one's paying any attention to Elliot or Mr. Fineman, either. Mr. Fineman is just standing there with his heart-attack face, looking worn-out and mad. It's too bad he's not a Buddhist because it seems as if he could use a trip to the ashram. I guess he still doesn't realize that nobody ever goes as far as my mother, it's not even a question, but after a few minutes spent pondering this, his shoulders slump as he finally gets the picture. Then he just turns around and limps out the door. He waves to Elliot to follow.

But Elliot doesn't go with him. Instead he makes his way toward our platform with a hunched walk. *He's* still wearing his cap. He comes right to the edge of the table and signals to me. I crouch, praying he can't see up my skirt. Elliot looks up at me with an intensity no boy has ever had for me; he stares right at me with those big green-brown eyes until my skin floats away from my bones. He opens his mouth, and for a split second I have the crazy idea that he's going to blurt out his Bar Mitzvah speech, which, he explained in class, begins with the traditional phrase: "Today I am a man."

Instead, he hisses a single word: "Yuck-O."

Then he spins around and struts away.

For about one second, I wish I could leave with him. He could be my boyfriend, and he'd take me away, and I'd never be subjected to a Mommy Binge again. But in the next second, I realize I detest him more than anything. So I decide to do something I've never done before: I scream. The sound comes up from my stomach and out of my mouth and billows into the room like a cloud of ant poison. I scream the strongest word I can think of, the word that will destroy him. I scream *Smelliot.*

It rises through the rafters of Brando's restaurant and hangs there. Elliot twitches as if he's been pierced by a dart. The crowd hushes for a second; time slows. Everyone is looking at me. All heads are swiveled in my direction. Suddenly, miraculously, I am the center of attention—me, Yoko, on the first day that I'm teenager—and it's wonderful. It's warm and sparkly and I love it.

Then everything speeds back up to normal and Elliot gives me one last sneer before skulking out the door.

My mother barely glances at me. She just says God, there goes that obnoxious runt of a Billy, and I climb down from the table and say yeah, I hate that stupid Billy. I choke back a glass of champagne, then call the waiter over and tell him to pour me more. He gives me the you-poor-thing look and I shoot back my mother's you-miserable-peon glance. I try to light a cigarette. I think maybe I'll be like her now that I'm becoming a woman. I'll be ferocious and loud and push us over the edge until we both fall into that terrible pit on that terrible island with the bloodthirsty dinosaurs. We'd live there together, the two of us, in the land of Too Far. Everywhere else, I'm an orphan.

My mother hands me a little box tied up with a ribbon. All the people milling around gather closer and say open it, open it. Inside are a pair of earrings—long daggers with rubies in the handle, just like the ones my mother is known for, the ones she wears on the *Plague of Filigree* CD cover. I take them out of the box and hold them up to the light while everyone says aren't they pretty! Just like your mother's! Aren't you a lucky girl! I say yes, yes I am, I'm very lucky, and take a drag off my cigarette and start coughing and feel sort of sick but I'm sure I can get over that. I slip the wires into my earlobes. They feel strange at first but after a minute or two I start to get used to it.

HABITS AND HABITAT OF THE
SOUTHWESTERN BAD BOY

None of this would have happened, none of this mess with Walter and the bad boy and the sandwich and the cow, if I'd been able to find a time that would have me. For a while, I seriously considered the 1980s. I have big hair naturally and I've always felt jaunty wearing those boots that turned into socks at the top. But I decided that only rocker chicks with frosted hair and bustiers yellowed by cigarette smoke were able to pull that off, and I was too uptight for that look. Then I believed my time to be the 1920s. I wore sleeveless shifts and made an effort to express myself through flowing movements, like Isadora Duncan. Too much gin and a day spent vomiting into the commode suggested that the 1920s were not going to embrace me, either.

I finally gave up. If a time wasn't going to have me, I wasn't going to waste my time pursuing one. Of course, whenever one gives up a fond hope, a hole springs open in the empty space. My life, a moth-eaten sweater, was filled with such holes. And so when my dear friend Walter turned to me and said, "Holy Toledo. Check it out. Bad boy at two o'clock," I turned, I looked, and I saw. I saw the bad boy.

The grim lesson I'd learned, in renouncing my search for a time that would have me, is that the only time is now, and it is impossible to inhabit now. For me, now is debased and embarrassing. Now is a limerick where everything rhymes with *pants*. The bad boy was bizarrely beautiful and young, with a pink bloom in his cheeks. You could almost see the desperation rising from him like the puff of dirt that enveloped Pig Pen in *Peanuts* cartoons. In his clothing, his fluid movements, the thick curtain of hair—for him, now was a sonnet. He could probably name three or four presidents, tops. Walter and I stared. The bad boy took a long drag from his cigarette, broodingly, his mouth pursed in a rock star pout. O, I thought, O that I might be a carcinogen within that deep-sucked breath!

The boy got up and lurched across the café. Walter and I watched him openly; we watched him the way we might track the antics of a squirrel in a park. He grabbed an ashtray and went weaving back to his seat.

"Three sheets," Walter noted, and cocked a brow.

We tittered. How naughty. Weeks earlier, to kill some time, we'd filled out sex surveys for a semi-risqué magazine, and in the space after "What is your favorite sexual fantasy?" Walter knew I had written: "Drunken teenage boys."

The boy ignored his cup of coffee and poked at a set of keys in front of him with distressed concentration, like an obsessed crow. On the basis of this, I guessed that he must be sixteen, with a new license and his mom's gleaming, innocent Saturn in the lot, waiting to be wrecked. I was probably only a few years younger than his mother, as was Walter, my friend and social escort, though we were not of parental ilk. We were easily distracted and underemployed. I sold low-fat scones to espresso joints and Walter worked in a bookstore. When we weren't doing those things, we wrote poetry, smoked cigarettes, and painted the insides of our apartments "interesting" colors like "Unagi" and "Loam." Walter had found *his* time: the 1940s. He wore smoking jackets and a pencil-thin mustache. At the bookstore, he glided through the aisles with the air of a bemused sophisticate. Patrons were afraid to ask him questions for fear of an acerbic reply.

"Look at him," I said.

Walter was already looking—at the adorable bangs, the long-lashed eyes, the restless feet. "The little buckaroo," he said.

"No one understands him."

"No," he agreed.

"Do you think he would, you know, *go* somewhere with us?" I gave him a significant look. He gave me a look in return. It said: "Are you psycho?" but with a subtext of prurient interest. I felt the stirrings of a conspiracy—about what, I wasn't clear. About the boy, I guess, the beautiful, shit-faced bad boy. He couldn't possibly be allowed to drive himself home.

"Our best chance," Walter said, "is if he's impressed by the fact that we're poets."

We laughed again, with more tension this time. We really were poets, or at least attempting to be. Over his desk, Walter kept a list of all the journals that had published his work. He was up to twenty. Over my desk, I kept a list of all the journals that had published my poetry, if you can call two names a list. That the boy would be impressed by this or anything at all appeared unlikely. Words in particular were a long shot, considering his T-shirt, which seemed to be from a foreign country where English was admired rather than understood. It said: "Do To Others As Others Have To You Be."

The bad boy noticed our interest and began to stare back. I tried a smile.

"What?" he blurted.

Walter and I traded amazed glances. It was as if a bunny rabbit had spoken.

"We were admiring your nail polish," Walter tried, in a suave, lying tone.

"Oh, yeah," said the boy, looking at his hand, "it's 'Savagery.'" He clawed the air with mock ferociousness. "It's new."

"Of course it is," Walter said, with an indulgent grin. It occurred to me that he might like the boy, too. And by like, I mean *like* like.

———

"Question!" screamed the boy. The three of us were sitting in the capacious front seat of my 1957 Chevy Bel Aire acquired during a brief, meaningless flirtation with the fifties. Below our feet zipped the ribbon of I-19 that stretched from Tucson to the Mexican border, past road signs that, in some incomprehensible burst of optimism, were calculated in metric.

"Answer!" yelled Walter. He and the boy gripped 40s. With the extra alcohol and the rush of air through the windows, the bad boy seemed to have boomeranged out of his brood into an edgy mania. It was as though he'd just been released from a room where they administered horrible tests.

"No, wait   no. Question! What do you get if you cross Lassie with a pit bull?"

His thigh fell heavily against mine, and when the breeze shifted, I could smell the bad-boy aroma of lemons and dirt. I gave him a sideways glance. His cheekbones were drop dead but his eyes were glazed. He was, I had to admit, utterly blotto.

"Cross them how?" I teased. "Do you mean crossbreed them?"

"Or cross Lassie, make-Lassie-mad-cross her?" Walter was babbling. He'd regressed, the way he did around boys he liked, mixing babiness with his innate sophistication until he became like a very suave ten-year-old. He giggled. I wondered if he thought he was on a date with the bad boy, with me as a chaperone. Whereas I thought of it more as kidnapping.

"No, come on," he protested, "you know what I'm saying! Just, like, *cross* them. Together."

"Oh," I said. "Okay. I see." Then I reached over and tousled his hair. What the hell. "What do you get?"

"Some type of bitch," Walter mumbled to the side mirror.

I ignored this. The bad boy didn't answer, either. He'd faded out of the debate and was pawing at the radio, trying, I suppose, to find some of the music of today. He popped us away from Peggy Lee on my oldies station. *Is that all there is?* she was wondering. It was hot in the car. One of the many problems of devoting oneself to the Eisenhower era was that air-conditioning was seen as an impossible luxury. As if in agreement, the boy bent an elbow over the top of his head and pulled his T-shirt clean off.

Walter and I looked at each other. That look, I believe, was a combination of shock, lust, and mutual panic, garnished with a sprig of deadly competition. There we were, speeding toward the border with a half-naked, underage boy pressed between us. It made me think of Audubon's painting of pintail ducks, wherein a pair of waterfowl lunge across a vacant, primordial landscape, beaks hanging open, both of them straining with every quill toward a single yellow fly, hanging like a dollop of custard at the top of the frame.

We drove on, flanked by low mountains and parched desert plants. The boy had given up on the radio and the Chevy filled with the sound of wind. In the café, we'd offered the bad boy an adventure and he hadn't thought twice, brushing back his bangs and squinting up at us. "Okay," he said, "let's rally." We had simply volunteered to take him on an expedition to see a giant cow skull.

After a while, the bad boy blurted, "A dog that rips off your hand, then goes and runs for help."

Everything wonderful had already died off. That was my feeling about it. Secretly, without telling Walter, I believed I might have located my time—the first half of the nineteenth century. That was when John James Audubon roamed the American continent, killing anything feathered. He killed then drew virtually every bird there was, and they had them all then. Audubon witnessed flocks of now-extinct passenger pigeons so vast they blackened the sky for hours. He drew them on a lichen-covered branch, a pair of slender birds with blue-tipped feathers. The girl bird is thrusting her beak into the boy bird's mouth in a moment of languorous instinct. Back then Indians picked berries on the ground where my apartment is and the Santa Cruz River flowed through Tucson year-round, fed by a prehistoric lake percolating through the desert floor. Now the river is a gravel trough, drained by golf courses and copper mines and neat little flower beds.

The giant cow skull had once been a snack bar. It was about twenty feet high, including the horns. Hungry visitors had entered through the nasal cavity, but the interior had long since been boarded up and the glory of the skull could now only be viewed from the outside. We parked and climbed out onto the packed dirt. We were right off the highway, in the middle of a lonely stretch of desert, at the start of a little road that led to a microscopic town called Sin Vacas, which translates to "Without Cows" in Spanish.

"Heavens," intoned Walter. "There seems to be a freakishly large cow skull over there."

The boy swayed on his feet and informed us that he had to pee. He stepped to the side of the car and did just that, on my tire. Walter and I wandered away and stared solemnly into the distance. When he was finished, the boy zipped up and began to walk toward us. His pants were slipping off his hips so that a crescent of boxer shorts showed above his waistband. His stomach was flat and his skin was tawny brown. The boy's shadow slipped into the gap between Walter's shoulders and mine. He had a last-minute chance to reach for me—I held my breath—but no, he stumbled toward Walter, drunker than ever, stretching his arms up over his head. Then he leaned in, and, with the open mouth so indicative of messy teenage kissing, crushed his lips to Walter's.

Reserved, suave Walter just *went* for it. He ground himself into the boy. He abandoned himself. I stood there, mesmerized, staring at their mouths as they made out, interested and repelled in equal measure. I reminded myself that I was striving to be a nineteenth-century lady, and with this in mind, I managed to walk across the lot and climbed into the car. The sun was low in the sky and the shadows of knife-edged agaves stretched over the ground. Light tumbled through the windshield into the Chevy. I thought that maybe the fifties weren't so bad after all. Anything seemed preferable to the depravity of now.

After a while, I heard an electronic wheezing coming from the backseat. I followed the noise to a phone in the boy's backpack.

"Hello?" said a woman's voice.

"Yes?"

After a pause, the woman said, "Where the fuck is Zach?"

"One moment, please."

I ferried the phone across the dirt. By the time I arrived, the bad boy was being very bad indeed. He had Walter pressed up beneath the cow's eye socket, mashed against a plate of faux bone. Clothes were falling off. I ignored this and tapped the boy on the shoulder.

"What?" he snapped.

I waved the phone. "It's your mother."

The boy looked at me with hating eyes. I have to admit I loved him in a sick way at that moment—O youthful rebellion, O reckless spirit! It was a brief, fleeting instant, I knew. I could scrawl poems until my fingers bled but there was no way to capture something like that. It would slip away: he'd grow up and become a real estate broker or an alcoholic or both. The window of opportunity to live a life of pure rage is very brief.

He took the phone. "Yeah?" he said, in a sulky tone. Then, flatly: "I don't know," and then, with anger: "I *said* I don't know," and then, with a rising note of distress: "I don't have to tell you everything I'm doing." Finally, just like the classic song, he proclaimed, "You don't own me!"

He jabbed off the phone. When I refused to take it back, he placed it on the ground and stepped away. He dug his hands into his hair; he rolled his eyes from side to side. What we were witnessing was a display of pure adolescent agony. It was awesome, it was fascinating, yet I only got to observe it for a moment, because then the boy turned, and with an easy, athletic gait, sprinted off into the desert.

Walter and I looked at each other with disbelief. For a second the ember of our camaraderie flared to life. Then I watched as it doused itself in Walter's eyes.

"Oh my God!" he commented. He patted his hair, smoothed down his pencil-thin mustache, and with an awkward, stiff-armed sprint, dashed off after the boy.

I didn't even know what this was. We smoked, we cracked wise, we drank coffee so strong we could stand spoons in it. In seven years, I'd never seen Walter *run*.

I lingered by the cow skull, walking in circles. The sun was sinking and everything was turning salmon pink. After a while the phone squeezed out another chirp from where it rested on a pile of rocks. Only a fool couldn't see where things were heading. Soon we wouldn't have real birds. We'd have avian simulators activated by motion detectors placed along a nature path with a corporate sponsor; to enter, you'd slide your card.

I decided to leave the phone to its ringing and walked into the desert in its last, fading hour. I believed that this was what Audubon would have done, though probably not in flip-flops. I could see no trace of Walter or the boy. I had to make my way carefully, watching out for cacti and other thorned plants. It hadn't rained in months, and everything was shrunken and yellow. I, personally, wasn't well acquainted with the outdoors, but I was willing to learn. I walked over a rise into a shallow arroyo. I rounded a knot of mesquite and found myself staring into the huge, syrupy eyeballs of a small cow.

"Hello," I said.

The cow nibbled a clump of brush.

"There's a snack bar made out of your bones around the corner."

The cow regarded me. It switched its tail; it allowed a fly to crawl on the membrane around its eyes. I saw that it was still a baby cow, adorable and sweet, and I cooed to it before I edged closer and threw my arms around its neck. It was warm and dusty and smelled like a dirty horse. I loved the cow. The cow was my consolation prize.

We stayed that way for a while, the cow and I, until flies started to crawl on my face and I stepped back in alarm. Somehow, it seemed, I'd engaged in some sort of imprinting ritual with the cow, because as I walked away it followed, straining toward me with an awkward, head-bobbing walk. It had a look of intense cow-need on its face, and in case I didn't understand, it began to make a loud, guttural moan that clearly meant *never leave me*.

"Go away," I told it. "I'm not your mommy."

I scrambled up the side of the arroyo with the cow at my heels. When that didn't work I threw rocks at it. And when that didn't work, I ran.

━━━━━

Night was falling. In the west, the sky clung to the palest wisp of pale blue like Isadora Duncan clinging to the last thread of her scarf. I'd returned to the car. I sat on the upholstery, which was still warm from the sun, and watched the calf nuzzle the tires. Every few minutes, it put its face to the window and slobbered; I finally had to gun the engine and honk the horn until its eyes rolled back and it skittered away in what I assumed was bovine terror.

Finally, when it was almost dark, Walter strolled into view. Behind him staggered the boy, his head hanging on his neck like an old sack. He seemed a whole lot less manic and bad than he had earlier, and a lot more tired and young. I have to admit, I still couldn't take my eyes off him. In the gathering dark his bone structure was more perfect, his silhouette even more luscious than I remembered. He truly was a rare specimen, gorgeous and doomed, like the Roseate Spoonbill, a rare shore feeder once plentiful on the Florida coast. Audubon's portrait shows a lone bird in full post-party dishevelment, with hot pink plumage and bloodshot eyes, wandering in a swamp beneath gathering storm clouds. The poor thing looks as though it should be clutching a bagful of condom wrappers.

"Are you okay?"

"Oh, probably not," said Walter.

The boy was still drunk or exhausted or both. I was sure Walter had done something to him, something naughty, but I wasn't about to ask what. They got in the car and we drove back to civilization in silence. Walter smoked cigarettes and stared out the side window into the night. He wouldn't look at me. The boy slept behind us in the backseat. After a while the city lights reappeared and we coasted off the highway.

When we stopped at a light, I turned to Walter. "You didn't have to leave me there," I said.

"It's not like I made you wait."

"Please. You knew I liked him."

He took a drag off his cigarette. "Yeah. I knew you wouldn't really do anything with him, either."

"You don't know that," I said. "You have no idea what I'd do."

Walter squinted off into the mysterious veil of the night. "My God," he said, "look how they spelled 'sandwiches.'"

There was a coffee shop on the opposite side of the intersection. The marquee said: "Fresh Sandwhiches Daily."

"I think I like it better that way."

"So do I," said Walter.

The light changed and I pulled into the intersection. Walter, meanwhile, dug around in the boy's backpack and pulled out a book that said "math" on the cover—not algebra or geometry—just "math." The boy's address was scrawled in a psychotic hand inside. Walter thought it was in the Sam Hughes neighborhood, so I turned the Chevy around and headed that way. It turned out the boy lived in a nice area, on a block of bungalows built in the 1930s. Looking at those little porches, I could almost picture men from the old days in fedoras, sitting on metal chairs, slowly dying of lung ailments.

We idled to a stop in front of a beige and white house. It was brightly lit, with some shrubs and a little rectangle of lawn in front.

"C'mon, kiddo." Walter poked the boy in the arm. "End of the line."

The boy looked at us blankly, then rolled over and burrowed his face into the upholstery. "Nooo," he moaned.

We opened the rear doors and went around to prod him. I tried to lift his head. It flopped back onto the seat as though there were neither muscles nor tendons within. Walter finally got a grip on the boy's arms and hauled him headfirst from the Chevy. He balanced him on the curb, half in the car, half out, until I came around from the other side and helped prop him up.

"Where are we?" he said.

"We're home!" I said brightly. This seemed to inspire the boy to begin a low, constant moaning.

We'd walked him halfway to the front door before his knees crumpled and he slithered to the grass, which was wet, from the sprinklers, I suppose. He crawled on his belly for a few feet then gave up and sprawled out in a twisted heap. He paused, retching a little.

"Hey," said Walter, bending over and patting him on the face. "Hey, little guy. Upsadaisy. Come on. Let's rally!"

The boy's eyes slid open. He stared at Walter as though he were trying to place him. Then he groaned, "I love you."

Walter looked from the house to the boy to the Chevy, then back again. "Oh my God," he said.

"What do you want to do?"

"I don't know." He seemed baffled. "I mean, we can't stay here, and we can't dump him."

The boy lay on his stomach, damp, panting, and oddly flat to the ground. *Dump him.* It sounded so light, so breezy. O breezy day.

"Yeah," I said, "Let's do that. Let's just go."

"No," moaned the boy, "wait."

I sighed. I suppose he was having a life crisis. I suppose he'd experienced his first blow job or similar sexual episode while he was with Walter and now he expected us to be as concerned about it as he was. All that rage, all that confusion, all that love. What a mess. Someone should have warned him not to get in a car with a couple of poets. All we wanted was to get home and write about him.

Walter looked at the boy. "Really? You want to leave him here all . . . twisted?"

"Yes," I said. "Yes I do."

The edge of a smile appeared at the corners of Walter's mouth. Just like that, I felt our camaraderie flare back to life. For once I felt very of-the-moment, very now. I didn't have to wait for him to agree. We were already jogging away from the house, toward the car. Walter tossed me his lighter, and I managed to torch the end of a cigarette just as I sprang open the door to the driver's seat. The night was warm and the lights of the city sparkled around us, better than stars.

I got a glimpse of the bad boy in the rearview mirror as we pulled out. Audubon's portrait would have shown him rearing up, his knees digging into the grass while a stain on the front of his shirt glowed a hard, noxious yellow. His mouth would be open as though he's about to utter his cry, the cry of the Southwestern Bad Boy—perhaps "fuck it" or "motherfucker." Audubon would have done a fine job capturing his beauty, the outlines precise and crisp, the colors vivid and true, painting him with the remarkable care he took with all his subjects, those poor birds, so beloved and used. It's a shame he had to kill them, but how could he have drawn them, otherwise? Nothing with any life it in could ever hold still long enough to render. The bad boy, for example, was already half out of his yard, stumbling after us.

Walter chewed a nail. "Does this thing go any faster?"

"Yes," I said, "yes it does."

I pressed my foot to the gas, and the engine, that marvelous machine, hurled us into the future.

THE LAND OF PAIN

You go for a walk and during the walk something happens: you trip, you fall, you dive off a cliff; you crash, you twist, you type for hours, you age. When you get home, you notice that your house looks slightly different than when you left—mushier, if that's possible, with misaligned corners. You open the door and are surprised to find a foil banner hanging over the mantle.

It says: *Welcome to the Land of Pain.*

So you go to the doctor and the doctor has you follow the standard management protocol (ice/rest/exercise/pills/ignore). When that doesn't work you go for the aggressive therapy intervention (surgery/pills/rest/ignore). Unfortunately, that doesn't work either, and one bright afternoon, the doctor and her entire staff sit you down and explain that you've basically reached the end of the line. Your options are (1) nothing, or (2) the brainless clone.

You're trying to be jaunty about this, upbeat and optimistic, and so opt for the brainless clone. Oh, they just call her that—she's not really brainless. She has a wee, reptilian brain stem that attends to her motor skills, her bodily functions, her ambulation and self-care and whatnot. She can be trained to do tricks and loves chocolate. When they pull her out of the vat, she is well formed and healthy and everybody is exceedingly pleased with her, though personally you're freaked out to see this little you, this exact genetic replica of yourself (only much younger, of course, and with no brain save a reptilian brain stem). But you're also excited, trembling with hope, because these brainless clones are state of the art and the next big thing and for the good of humankind and a leap forward for science and all that.

You take her home and put her on accelerator, a clear goo that comes in a green squeeze bottle and is, they've told you, sort of like plant food. With this stuff dripped into her food, she grows at a brisk pace. You ignore her for a while, but as she starts to enter various awkward stages that you recognize from your own girlhood, you haul her out of the cage and cart her off to lessons. You make her study ballet. You force her to do yoga. You have her practice in padded rooms, far from any of the known entrances, pitfalls, chutes, or trapdoors that lead to the Land of Pain. You want her graceful. You want her flexible and strong.

Because she's your ticket out, sweetheart. She's your luxury cruise to a tropical island.

Sometimes you sit and watch her to see if you can catch her growing. You drip extra gobs of accelerator into her food (though this is not recommended). Her routine goes like this: in the cage, eat, sleep, defecate, stare blankly. Out of the cage: plié, relevé, sun salute, headstand, stare blankly. The legality of the deal is that she needs to grow to adulthood before you can have the operation. This is the operation where they take out your big, thinking-and-feeling brain that possesses humanity and patch it into the smooth cavity inside her head, into that flesh-lined bucket (thwack!), so that from that moment on, your consciousness exists inside a pain-free, healthy, twirling and leaping body, identical to your own (except younger, and not in pain). What do they do with your old body? They use it for experiments.

As of yet, no one has successfully undergone the brain transfer operation.

But, they assure you, it's only a matter of time.

Anyway, you enjoy just hanging out and watching your clone practice. She's got those buck teeth and short little legs you had at her age. You cut her hair so she has the dorky bangs you once had. If you toss her a chocolate kiss she'll do a pirouette. For a whole candy bar, she'll attempt a solo from *Swan Lake.*

In the meantime, you undergo a series of medical tests in an attempt to better understand the painful region. The region is explored with needles in an effort to isolate the painful spot. If they can pinpoint the spot, say the doctors, then they will be able to discuss interim treatment strategies with you. And if they cannot reach it with the needles they have tried so far, they will just have to try some longer ones.

You say: Any luck yet with the old brain switcheroo, Doc?

Doc says: We're close, very close.

The brainless clone continues to ripen. Though the process is accelerated, it nevertheless takes several years, years you spend languishing in the Land of Pain: eating grapes, watching movies, popping pills, worsening, enduring therapies, pretending you are not in the Land, and so on. The brainless clone barrels into adolescence, a time you spent slumping through the halls of junior high with a book clasped before your breasts. She looks better than you ever did, clear skinned and white toothed, and in her own way she's clever too. She's figured out how to open her cage with her feet. You wonder, why not with her hands? Ah, well, they don't call them brainless for nothing!

You try to get her to stay in her cage but you're not much of a disciplinarian. You're supposed to squirt her with water when she's bad, but she looks so bewildered when you do, so wounded and damp, that you give it up. You're also supposed to be able to direct her movements by shining a flashlight in her face (this is also the way you wrangle Sea Monkeys, you've been told) but this only makes her fold into a weeping ball, presenting such a startling replica of your own miserable adolescence that you toss the flashlight in the trash and give her a cookie. You vaguely wonder exactly who is training who.

The result of this is that the brainless clone gains the run of the house. She twirls around all the time. If she walks, she walks on her tiptoes. She takes up more space than you ever imagined possible. It's as though a tiny, windup jewelry box dancer has been turned into a giant adolescent monster through the ingestion of radioactive produce. You dodge around her swanlike arms and contemplate how you were never that graceful or slender or pretty. Complex feelings ensue.

You and the other members of the study have been advised not to give names to your brainless clones. Researchers come to the house every couple of months to check up on her progress, her care and feeding, your compliance and mental health. As soon as they leave, you take off her scrub suit and dress her in a silk tutu. You've named her Princess Fifi.

At home, your answering machine says: "Hello, you have reached THE LAND OF PAIN," over a background of thundering organ music. None of your callers find this funny or even particularly comprehensible. It looks as if you've failed at the long tradition of cracking jokes in the face of adversity and thus signaling that you're a tough cookie and a brave little bumblebee and a trooper and all that. The truth is you're getting sick of pretending that the Land of Pain is not a sad and lonely place. You're sick of acting as though losing your old, pain-free body is anything less than entirely heartbreaking.

Things could be worse, the doctors are fond of reminding you. Chin up! It's just pain, it won't kill you. You decide this is typical of the kind of thoughts people have when they do not live in the Land of Pain. Your thoughts run more along the lines of, why not do a few good deeds to boost your karma, then throw in the towel? Maybe in the next life, you'd get a better body. Unfortunately, things look bad all around out there: war, genocide, children with machine guns, rape and plunder and tyranny and epidemics. You don't want to be reincarnated into one of those bodies.

Anyway, you don't believe in reincarnation.

The brainless clone keeps twirling between you and the TV when you're trying to watch the horrible news programs that remind you how much worse things could be. You try to kick her out of the way and get mud all over your socks. Ever since she learned how to crawl through the doggy door, she's been ripping her tutus and dragging them in the dirt. She's been climbing trees and running through the sprinklers, getting sunburned and collecting scars that you'll eventually have to explain, once you inhabit her body. What's more, your assistive animal (which you obtained after watching a videotape of a sweet, serious collie picking up coins with her mouth) considers your leather armchair a chew toy and has reduced half of it to pulp. Somehow you had the idea that the assistive animal was going to be a terrific help. You had built up in your mind a whole fantasy scenario in which this wonderful assistive animal would do all the things you found difficult—she would organize your shoes, pick up coins off the floor, make the bed with her little teeth and paws, dragging the sheets up carefully over the mattress (good dog!) and stuffing a pillow into a clean pillowcase with her snout. Then she'd curl up at your feet while you relaxed in a specially designed, inexpensive contraption that suspended you in a warm, soothing fluid, relaxed and completely pain-free.

When you try to scoot the chair away, the dog sinks her teeth into the other side, growling happily, proposing a superfun game of tug-of-war. You muse on the fact that something like twenty-three muscles govern that wagging tail. And it's obvious none of them hurt.

───

You take your medicine and sack out in front of the television (which you can only really watch when you manage to nudge the pirouetting brainless clone into a corner). Now is the hour when citizens on talk shows tell their tragic stories in the second person, saying *you you you* about all the bad, traumatic, unfortunate experiences in their lives ("You just feel so betrayed when you see that little panda pulling a gun") as though they have a genetic defect that prevents them from using the pronoun "I." This is sloppy and angers the grammar and usage thug in you. You've concluded that citizens telling their tales of adversity find the second person compelling because "you" is impersonal and removed, yet somehow includes everyone in its scope ("It could be you staring down the barrel at that panda bear next, sweetheart!") whereas "I" is an orphaned baby doe blinking in a dark forest.

"You are always in pain," for example, is a more manageable utterance than the direct, final "I am always in pain."

At nightfall, you can't find the assistive animal anywhere. Finally, you locate her curled up in the cage with the brainless clone, nose tucked under her tail. They adore each other. And you, you my friend, are filled with jealousy.

———

You go to the doctor and the doctor says, Rate your pain on a scale of one to ten, with one being negligible and ten being the worst pain you can possibly imagine, such as—you brace yourself here—*surgery on your internal organs without anesthesia!* The doctor asks this every time you visit, and every time it horrifies you. You imagine an awful knoll in the Land of Pain where doctors remove livers and kidneys without the benefit of anesthesia while brainless clones dance to the soothing strains of waiting-room music. In the foreground, assistive animals grab twitching organs in their mouths and run off to bury them.

You are not being a brave little bumblebee.

What's more, a few minutes later, you start crying there on the greenish exam table because the doctor is telling you they have completed the brainless-clone study and have concluded that, unfortunately, they cannot, at this time, transfer human brains from one body to another. And there is very little else they can do to help you. When you start to cry, the doctor takes a deep breath and, with a kind of angry glee (similar to when the assistive animal picks up a coin and runs around the house, while you attempt to chase), starts to recite, in detail, a list of all her patients who are worse off than you. She describes neighborhoods in the Land of Pain more burned out and dangerous than you ever dreamed of, hellish vistas where the afflicted and wracked limp through the streets in hailstorms while gobbling Oxy-Contin and forgetting who the president is. Phantom Limb Pain. Fibromyalgia. Double Carpal Tunnel (with a cherry on top), Stiff Person Syndrome. You sniffle contritely and feel a weird, toxic gratitude that goes: Thank God. Thank God I'm only as fucked up as I am and not as fucked up as those other people.

The doctor says, We understand you have a choice when choosing Lands, and we'd like to thank you for choosing to spend the safest part of your journey here, in the Land of Pain.

———

Geographically speaking, the Land of Pain is a subcontinent of the World of the Sick. The World of the Sick is a nifty, parallel universe that exists inside the World of the Well. The curious fact is that while most citizens of the World of the Well don't even realize that the World of the Sick exists, *all* the inhabitants of the World of the Sick know about the World of the Well. The Sick live among the healthy like spies, pod-people, or day-walking vampires: different, afraid, and isolated, and like spies, pod-people, and day-walkers, the Sick who can manage to mingle with the Well reflexively disguise their identity. And you, with your white picket fence and your neatly trimmed lawn in the Land of Pain, you are no different. There's no little chair on your license plate. You look normal, you are able to leave the house for hours at a time, you've tried to pass yourself off as hunky-dory.

But now everyone knows, because in her maturity the brainless clone follows you everywhere. She won't let you out of her sight. She bellows like a water buffalo if you stray too far from her, she bellows so fiercely that you think it's possible that she'll go on forever. She's inconsolable and stubborn and unpredictable and, thanks to years of physical training, she possesses astonishing stamina. Rather than fight it, you do what you've always done and cave in. You take her everywhere with you. She trots at your side, grunting. She won't wear anything now but soiled tutus and you have to attach her to your wrist with a tether because, well, she doesn't exactly have a brain. You find the whole spectacle humiliating: she's an idea whose time has passed, a relic of a failed era. It's as though you're a weird person carrying around an eight-track player and truckin' to disco. Certain kids find this cool and follow at a distance, trying to affect her distracted, zombie stance. Far worse are the religious zealots, who bother you constantly. They know where you live. They mobilize when you go to the doctor or the supermarket. They surround your car and chant: *Even without a cerebellum / That young lady's going to heaven!* The nuts are convinced she has a soul (though she has no brain), and even though you have to get a restraining order against them, you're secretly inclined to agree.

So you walk around with this big, grunting, simple ballerina following you, and everyone knows there's something so wrong with you that you once actually contemplated having your brain taken out and put into someone else's body, which in fact isn't the worst part. The worst part is when everyone goes, Oh! She's so cute! Were you ever that cute? There, tethered to you with a piece of coiled plastic, is your lost youth and vitality: a pretty ballerina, arm raised, back arched, foot aiming toward the sky. She's a poet of the body, ignited with life, and despite her lack of brain, you're in awe of all she has.

———————

A friend says to you, Oh, these people take them to live on a farm. They have a farm for the brainless clones out in the country where they get to run around in the fresh air, and there are orchards and meadows and pet bunnies and they're well cared-for and all that. A group of bran-eating hippies runs it—they do it for karma credits or energy wavelengths or something weird but reputedly not evil. A lot of the brainless clones are living there now. They have sing-alongs.

You say, Sounds fishy.

Your friend says, Yeah. Oh, but wait—the thing is they grow those pears there, the ones we used to get at the corner market. Remember those pears?

You remember. You used to stop at a little market and buy the most ravishing pears, sweet and crisp, and every time you did the proprietor would roar, You will be back for more of these pears! They were yellow-gold. You'd eat them in the park while the juice ran off your elbow. You went back again and again, just as the man predicted. It was the longest pear-season ever, and you were convinced it would never end.

But of course it did end, and you moved to another part of the city, and by chance wandered into the Land of Pain and forgot all about the pears, since you had other things on your mind.

So you take her to the farm. She wants to get off her leash and run around all the time now anyway. You bundle up her ballet slippers and her tutus and her bags of Brainless Clone Chow and push her into the backseat of the car and set off for the country. She keeps sticking her entire head out the window as you drive, making that grunting noise, so awful and familiar and constant. My God, you think, please make it stop.

When you arrive, she jumps out as soon as you open the car door. You give her a little kiss on her zombie brow and unclip the leash. She stands for a minute, sniffing the air, chest heaving, fingers trembling, then breaks into a dead run for the orchard. Her tutu is the cleanest you could find, a pink one, and the pears hang above her like yellow lanterns. Her arms unfurl as she reaches up and her fingertips graze the branches. Then she lifts a foot and begins to dance. She's a damn good dancer; breathtaking, really, like a scarf drifting through the air. You watch for a while, trying not to imagine all she could have been if she'd actually had a brain.

There are a couple dozen other brainless clones romping in the orchard too. They all look alert and healthy: they are eating pears, wrestling, singing snatches of camp songs, picking their noses, doing summersaults. It's sort of beautiful but also awful. What if their owners suddenly all showed up? What if they arrived with their crutches and wheelchairs and bad eyes and frozen joints and stood around (if they could stand) and watched (if they could watch) as their clones pranced and jumped and fell down and then got back up again? Really, it would be too much to endure.

The weird karma people appear and offer you a bowl of cereal. She's cute, they say. She'll like it here. Everything will be fine. You all stand awhile watching the clones horse around. Then they tell you that it's time to say good-bye.

Oh no, you say, no. You don't want to say good-bye.

They take away your bowl of cereal and look at you with gentle, patchouli-scented eyes. They tell you that it's good to say good-bye and that you really should.

But no, you argue. Hold it right there. Just who do they think they are, telling you to say good-bye? Let's be realistic here. There are things in life no one should have to say good-bye to. How can you say good-bye to your unbroken version, the good version, the one that dances? It's not fair! And how can it be that people don't get better? How can their pretty ballerinas dance away under the pears while their owners hobble home, on their feet, on their crutches, in their wheelchairs? Why did they have to wait until they were unable do the simplest things to realize that the simplest things were full of joy: taking a walk, picking a pear, lifting a child who says carry me.

So there it is. You don't want to say good-bye.

Chill out, say the weird karma people. Jesus. No one is making you do anything. You don't have to leave her here. But if you keep her she'll probably keep following you around, grunting. Furthermore (and here they look very sinister), they believe that the universe will be far more peaceful in its vibrations if you can manage to say good-bye. They stand there with their wispy ponytails and their heavy bags of granola, perhaps suitable for use as a weapon, so you decide to give it a try. You call out *good-bye little clone* in a small voice, without much conviction. *Bye-bye, Fifi.* You give your brainless princess a wave, but of course she's not looking at you. She's too busy dancing beneath the pears.

———

You accept a bag of cereal from the karma people and start to drive back to town. Your assistive animal sleeps in the backseat, twitching and whining, chasing rabbits or perhaps a flock of brainless clones. Somehow, though you're certain you didn't make any wrong turns, you end up on a strange, unrecognizable stretch of freeway. You realize that you're angry, very angry: wherever you are, you would like to know just how you ended up here! You'd demand to know, if only you could find someone to ask. At last a green, reflective sign rears up along the side of the road. It says: Next Exit: The Land of Pain.

You exit.

A CASE STUDY OF EMERGENCY ROOM PROCEDURE AND RISK MANAGEMENT BY HOSPITAL STAFF MEMBERS IN THE URBAN FACILITY

I.

Subject 525, a Caucasian female in her early to midtwenties, entered an emergency medical facility at around 11 P.M. presenting symptoms of an acute psychotic episode. Paranoia, heightened sensitivity to physical contact, and high-volume vocal emanations were noted at triage by the medical staff. The subject complained of the hearing of voices, specifically "a chorus of amphibians" who were entreating the subject to "pretty please guard the product from the evil frog prince." The staff reported that the subject's bizarre behavior was augmented by an unusual sartorial style, commenting that she was "an ethereal young woman wearing a Renaissance-type dress, with huge knots in her long, otherwise flowing hair." She was accompanied by a strange odor, tentatively identified as "cat urine."

During the intake interview, the subject volunteered the information that she had nasally inhaled "crystal," estimating that she had nasally inhaled (snorted) between 50 and 250 mg of "crystal" in the twenty-four hours prior to hospital admission. "Crystal," it was determined, is a slang term for methamphetamine, a central nervous system stimulant similar to prescription amphetamines such as Benzedrine. Methamphetamine is a street drug of abuse that has become popular in recent years due to its easy manufacture possibilities (Osborne, 1988). It is sometimes referred to by the terms *crystal, speed, zoomazoom,* and *go fast* (Durken, 1972). In a brief moment of lucidity, Subject 525 theorized that her psychotic state might be due to the large quantity of methamphetamine she had "snorted," and the staff agreed to put her in a "nice, quiet, white room" for a period of observation. The head resident thought it advisable to administer antipsychotic medication, but the subject, who by all accounts exhibited an uncanny amount of personal charm, prevailed on the staff to give her a can of beer instead.

II.

After approximately sixty minutes of observation, a member of the nursing staff noted that the subject had begun to complain that "a be-slimed prince" was causing certain problems for her, namely, "using copper fittings" and "not ventilating right." This "prince" was, as the nurse understood it, acting "all mean and horrible" concerning the manufacture of methamphetamine, which the subject had cheerfully volunteered as her occupation during the intake interview. The nurse, who was formerly employed in a federal prison and had considerable experience treating denizens of the demimonde, theorized that "Prince" might by a moniker used by the subject's "old man"; this was particularly likely, the nurse indicated, since the manufacture of methamphetamine is the customary province of "gangs" of motorcycle riders, who often use colorful nicknames as a way of asserting their "outsider" status in society (Ethel Kreztchner, R.N., 2002).

The nurse further asserted that this would explain why the subject had offered, at intake, only the name "Princess" and would indicate no surname. By then the hour had grown rather late, and as the emergency room was quiet, much of the staff gathered around the subject ("Princess"), who began to tell a lively tale of capture and imprisonment by a handsome but wicked "prince" who was, in fact, "an evil enchanter." The tradition of shape-shifting sorcerers is a familiar one in old German folk tales (Grimm, ca. 1812), though these tales have been widely regarded as fanciful narratives concocted to intimidate and control unruly juveniles (twelve and under) in diverse cultural contexts and are rarely considered historical evidence. Nevertheless, the Princess claimed that the Prince had captured her from an orphanage near Eloy, Arizona, where she had spent her days climbing trees in pursuit of nuts. Chasing butterflies, according to the subject, was another activity she enjoyed in her youth. But this all changed when a handsome young man approached the girl and offered her a pony made of candy. The pony was beautiful and delicious, and though the Princess wished to save it forever, she devoured it anyway. With every bite, the pony grew smaller. And with every bite, the handsome "young man" become more fearsome and wicked-looking.

The staff gathered close, listening with great interest. The Princess went on to indicate that the Prince/Sorcerer had bewitched her with the candy horse and had since imprisoned her in a prefabricated "home" near a foul-smelling landfill, where she was kept locked up in a "tin can with carpet taped over the windows." There, the Prince had prevailed on her to undertake the smelly and dangerous manufacture of methamphetamine by means of his sorcerer's power. All day long, the Princess said, she was forced to "boil down Mexican ephedrine in a triple-neck flask, bubble hydrogen through a stainless steel tank, or titrate ethyl ether out of lock-defrosting fluid, dressed only in filthy rags," while the Prince rode his shiny "hog" through tall pines in the mountains to the north of town. Or the Prince would "relax and kick back with a can of brew" while the Princess "slaved over a hot chemistry set." The only positive aspect of the experience, the Princess noted, was that she "cooked the best damn product in Arizona," a substance that was uncommonly potent and white, she said, with a "real clean buzz."

The Princess explained, in a sweetly chiming voice, that these endeavors were dangerous, particularly under the conditions imposed by the Prince, who habitually smoked marijuana cigarettes in the vicinity of fumes. She had survived because she was protected by a special angel, one with "gills" who could exist underwater or possibly "inside a solution." She referred to this angel as "Gilbert" (possibly "Gillbert") and noted that Gilbert appeared to her when she imbibed heavily of "the product." The manifestation of angels, seraphim, djinns and Elvis Presley is common during episodes of psychosis (Hotchkiss, 1969), and much of the staff believed that the Princess was describing an aspect of methamphetamine-induced hallucination. Others on staff found themselves strangely moved by the Princess's story of forced enslavement and the high-risk game of organic chemistry, and wondered if there might be some sort of truth to it.

The head resident, in particular, took an interest in the subject's case, indicating to researchers that he was "bored that night, as usual" and that he found the Princess "interesting." The resident further indicated that his prodigious academic success was based on his above-average intelligence, which was also "a curse" because it led him to feel a feeling of "boredom," and intolerance with all "the idiots around him," which, he made clear, also applied to the researchers gathering data on this case. Researchers in turn described the resident as rather "vain and haughty," or "arrogant," though most theorized that these traits covered up insecurity about his youth combined with a doomed romanticism undercut by a persistent tendency toward bitterness.

The Princess was exhibiting fewer symptoms of psychosis and had become quite comfortable in her surroundings, curling up in a nest of pillows "like a cat" (Overhand, 2002). She said that she loved the medical staff and was grateful to them for helping to save her from the evil Prince and the pungent squalor of methamphetamine manufacture. The head resident shuffled his feet and pointed out that the Princess herself had actually contributed to her own care by wisely seeking medical treatment when she felt overwhelmed by drug-induced psychosis, whereas a lot of "tweaked-out idiots" just went ahead and did something stupid or violent. Then the two stared awhile into each other's eyes.

It was then that the lateness of the hour was nervously remarked on by all, and several staff members complained that they had been on duty for an excessive length of time. The Princess made a "general comment" that her product could "give a person a little pick-me-up" that theoretically might make the staff members feel as though "they were operating at one hundred and fifty percent."

The staff was curious about the efficacy of the Princess's homemade methamphetamine, though their enthusiasm abated somewhat after a phlebotomist (a "pretty, plump girl who never wore any makeup and never smiled or said hello to nobody beneath her," according to the environmental control officer) recited aloud in a high and quavering voice a list of the possible effects of nasally inhaling methamphetamine, including "nervousness, sweating, teeth-gnashing, irritability, incessant talking, sleeplessness, and the obsessive assembling and disassembling of machinery" (PDR, 2002). Interest swelled again when the Princess pointed out that the young phlebotomist had mumbled while mentioning one of the chief effects of the substance: euphoria.

After that, the staff cleared from the small room where the Princess was being kept sequestered by herself, though occasionally a lone member would disappear inside, to emerge a few moments later wiping their nose and with eyes unusually wild. Such staff members were also observed tidying their work areas, peering into the mirror, smoking cigarettes, and talking to one another with great animation and enthusiasm but little content (Overhand, 2002). The receptionist was observed taking apart a telephone, so that she could "clean it." The overall effect was that the staff was unusually energetic and "happy" (see below).

III.

Shortly before dawn, several nurses returned to the Princess's bedside, where they adjusted the lighting in the small room so that a warm glow bathed the subject. They worked with combs to untangle the knots in the subject's hair. The head resident had entered the room as well, and kept his boyish face, so incongruous beneath his balding head, hunched toward his chest while he made notes in the subject's chart.

It was then that the subject began to speak softly about a set of ponies she had made out of old tires. The Princess explained how she had "freed" the ponies from the rubber with a cutting implement, and that a "herd" of such ponies hung from ropes in the trees around her prefabricated housing unit, where they blew back and forth in the breeze, bumping against each other with hollow thuds. They possessed the spirit of "running things," she explained, though they had no "legs to speak of." She could look at them and feel the feeling of "something wild and running away." The subject further explained that nasally inhaling or "skin popping" (subcutaneous injection of) methamphetamine gave her relief from a feeling that "nothing important would ever happen to her," and replaced it with the sensation that she was, like the ponies fashioned from discarded tires, something "wild and running away."

She indicated that these feelings of flight accounted for the only times that she ever truly felt like a princess.

IV.

The notes in the subject's chart at this point become "tiny and very, very neat," according to researchers (Plank et al., 2002). The notes themselves indicate that the subject was "an exceptionally attractive woman" and that the medical staff found her "enchanting." She was "like them but different—more perfect—yet at the same time more glassine and fragile." The chart noted that the subject had become sleepy, perhaps due to the fatigue that often follows the ingestion of methamphetamine (Nintzel, 1982). It was indicated that some members of the staff wished to allow her to sleep, while others had an urgent need to "pester her; to poke her in the leg with a stick over and over," to keep her awake.

Verbal accounts indicate that not all the members of the night staff were equally smitten with the subject. Several members demurred, in particular the phlebotomist, who commented that the subject was "a disgusting drug addict" who was "manipulative." She added that she hated men "who fall for those poor, lost creatures," even though such "creatures" were in the process of getting "exactly what they signed up for." The phlebotomist indicated that it was futile to try to help the subject, save medically, because the subject had freely chosen her own seedy destiny, despite her weird story of kidnapping, adding that "not everybody who suffers has a burning need to dramatize it with scarves and eyeliner."

V.

Videotapes from the security cameras in the waiting area provide a clear visual record of the intrusion that occurred at approximately 4:12 A.M. The tapes show a clean, tiled area violently rent by the shiny chrome form of a very large motorcycle (or "hog") piloted by the "Prince," who gained ingress by method of riding through the glass doors, where he continued to gun his motorcycle in circles through a reception area furnished with chairs, which became smashed. The "Prince" was reported to be a large, muscular male of indeterminate race sporting "a pair of sideburns as big as teacups." He was reportedly clad in "enough black leather to

denude several cows," though naturally it has not been determined how many cows would have been needed to provide the amount of leather the Prince was wearing. Much of
the hospital staff on duty also reported that the intruder had
a "tail, slimy and black, sort of like the tail of a tadpole."
Careful scrutiny of security videotapes does reveal the presence of a whiplike appendage dangling from the back of the
Prince's "hog," though the possibility that this might in fact
be a literal tail has been discounted by researchers, who have
chalked up this and several other aspects of the medical
staff's report to group suggestibility (Johansen, 2002). (For
example, the hospital staff also reported that the Prince had
"eyes that glowed red like coals" and that "lizards and snakes
slithered from his boots.")

It was reported that the Prince then parked his "hog" and
proceeded past the reception area, stalking the warrenlike
halls of the emergency treatment facility in his heavy boots,
scuffing the floor, screaming that someone had taken his
"woman," and wondering aloud, in a yelling tone, where he
could find his "kitten."

At this the Princess and hospital staff fled to a supply
closet, where they cowered, leaving the issue of how to
properly control the Prince open for resolution. It was
agreed that the police, as well as the hospital security guards,
should be alerted; it was lamented, however, that there was
no available phone in the supply closet and such action
would require someone to dash out into the hallway, where
the Prince was raging and overturning carts and smashing
his hammerlike hands into walls while eating candy re-

served for children who were unfortunate enough to wind up in the emergency room. The Princess, whose melodic voice was muffled due to the press of bodies in the supply closet, pointed out that the Prince possessed special evil magic powers and that anyone who challenged him must be good in heart and clever both, and carry with him or her a small silver bell, which the Princess kept on a chain around her neck.

As the destructive noises of the Prince's rampage became louder, the head resident indicated that he felt he should be the one to make an effort to save himself, the staff, and the once-psychotic but now quite sweet Princess. The staff was surprised to hear this, as they had never noticed any behavior related to bravery or even simple kindness on the part of the head resident. They continued to be surprised when they heard him say, in a quavering voice, that though it was true he might not be good-hearted, he certainly was *clever* enough, so why not give it a go? Everyone in the closet gave him a quiet but heartfelt round of applause. The Princess begged him to be careful and hung the bell around his neck with a trembling hand. She bestowed upon him a soft kiss as he slipped out the door.

The "rescue" of women by handsome, effeminate men is a staple of old folk tales, engineered to reconcile a young woman's inclinations towards feckless independence with the prevailing custom of marriage by casting the potential husband as really nice and sort of harmless and at the very least a whole lot better than the alternative of living with her fucked-up family (cf. *Cinderella*, Grimm, 1812). Despite the tradition of the effeminate male's triumph over the more sexual, "animal" challenger, it seemed uncertain to all present that the head resident could defeat the Prince using the tools at his disposal—a stethoscope, some pens, and a pager. It's difficult to determine, though, what kind of damage the resident might have been capable of inflicting with these devices, since, according to his own account, when confronted with the fierce and gruesome Prince, who "smelled like burning rubber and had white stuff hanging off his beard," he froze, then mutely raised a traitorous arm to point to the supply closet where the Princess and the rest of the staff were hiding.

The Prince wrenched open the door with a huge paw, and out popped the Princess.

According to the staff, the Princess screamed with a high-pitched yelp when the Prince grabbed her, smearing her lovely Renaissance-style dress with grease. The records note that the Prince and the Princess together presented quite an odd picture, one that brought to mind "a nightmare creature clawing a plate of petit fours" (Petix, 2002). The Princess is reported to have said, "It's okay," and, "No, but I want to go with him, really," and, "He's my old man!" in a tone of tense brightness, but the staff plainly did not believe her and theorized that she was simply trying to "appease her oppressor" in order to minimize the likelihood of domestic violence. Before the staff was able to contact the authorities, the Prince settled himself astride his hog and pulled the Princess up behind him.

The Prince and Princess roared out of the building and vanished into the night in a cloud of exhaust.

Conclusion

After the Prince and Princess had departed, the staff grumbled that the head resident had behaved "most cowardly," and complained that the Princess had been "sacrificed," to be "whisked off to a prefabricated house where everything is always fast and tinged with madness, or else dark and sad and falling asleep." Much of the staff argued that *something* should have been done to help the girl, though some felt it was the curse of the phylum *Princess* to be always at the mercy of one prince type or another, and that her best chance was to save herself, which seemed unlikely. The resident, for his part, quickly aligned himself with the phlebotomist, agreeing that the Princess was "just an addict" who had come in "exhibiting drug-seeking behavior anyway," and implying, in word and action, that drug addicts were by nature less than human and so deserved whatever nasty fate they got. Then he skulked off down a fluorescent-lit hallway with his hands shoved into his pockets.

Though he wore the silver bell around his neck to the end of his days.

YOUNG PEOPLE TODAY

Dear Flora,

I promised I would explain why, at this late point in life, I've taken to spending time with the young people, and I suppose your curiosity was piqued further by Ethel's report that I sat at a separate table with the college-aged hooligans at Tiffany's wedding and then was spotted outside with the smokers. To explain I feel I must tell the whole story from the beginning. I hope you'll bear with me, as you always have.

It all started when I hired a day laborer to take up the linoleum in my kitchen. I got the name from a bulletin board in the little health food store around the corner, and I found I liked the young fellow who came over, Andy Hassenfield. He was a guitar player, he said, for the rock and roll group The Rudimentary Organs. It was imperative, he explained, to include the word "The" in the title: The Rudimentary Organs. To him this was very important, because it imparted a kind of stiffness to the name he found pleasing to the ear. I know, it's tough to get. Kids today, these twenty-somethings, these Generation XYZ-ers, they like anything mixed up or backwards. They like shapeless old housedresses and terrible eyeglasses and the sickly shade of green our mothers painted their kitchens. If it's ugly, they think it's splendid. That's the first rule with these kids: if you don't understand what they're doing, or wearing, or talking about, just reverse it, and it starts to make sense.

I liked Andy so much I decided to keep him on for a while. I knew he probably smoked pipes of pot, and he came in some mornings complaining he felt hungover from drinking keg beer behind some location downtown where punk rock drug addicts cut their chests with shards of bottle glass while he banged on his guitar strings. The stories he told me! Sometimes I thought I should have presented a more disapproving countenance, but heck, he wasn't my son, and he was always prompt and efficient. And oh, Flora, he was one of those boys you just love having around the house. He was always saying "thank you" and "excuse me"—a big, tall boy with a sweet face and an entirely bald head that made my heart ache for him. It seems to me that in our day, boys didn't lose their hair at such a tender age. They did everything else earlier, went off to war or supported families, but at least their poor heads were padded with locks. Well, Andy was handsome, nevertheless, and he had one of those faces that couldn't hide a thing. Currents of wonder and hurt and satisfaction, even little eddies of deception, flowed across his face with such vividness that reading his mood was about as arduous as opening up the newspaper.

———

After he was finished with the linoleum, I decided to have him clean and paint the gutters, then reroof the shed. These were tasks that had to be done, anyway, and Andy seemed quite competent to perform them. He would arrive around 9:30 in the morning and sit with me for a while in the kitchen. I made him espresso coffee in that little Italian stove-top boiler my daughter gave me for Christmas. That was the year she put in the note that said: "Off to Bermuda to work on our tans!" I opened a window and Andy sat across from me in the breakfast nook, smoking clove cigarettes and apologizing for smoking in the house, even though I told him I didn't mind. We'd chat, sometimes for an hour or more. I wasn't used to such strong coffee then, and I'd find myself rattling on about abstract art, myth and symbol, the collective unconscious—all that crazy stuff we used to talk about in the old days before they tore down the Unitarian church.

Andy listened and talked about the things he was interested in himself. He told me about the pretty girls he liked who never seemed to like him back for more than a day or two, while storms of disappointment darkened his face. His stories had a structure that interested me. First they puzzled, then they edified. For example, one concerned traveling in a van with another rock and roll group named Clean Dirt. One evening Andy was too tired to help the other boys set up the equipment, and a rival musician from Clean Dirt expressed his anger at this by throwing Andy's shoes out of the van while it was moving. Andy explained that because of this, he had to walk around in his stocking feet for a week.

I asked, "Why didn't you buy yourself a new pair of shoes?"

"That's a good question." He looked into his clove cigarette, which made my house smell like an Indian spice market, and laughed a little. It wasn't a real belly laugh but more of a "heh, heh." He said, "I guess I was kind of *into* not having shoes. I was, like, into the total humiliation of it."

You see what I mean, about flipping things backwards? As I understood it, going without shoes caused Andy to feel ashamed, which in turn made him feel good. In this way, negative experiences are made positive. It takes some practice, but I believe anyone can get the hang of interpreting these reversals. Once I got the knack, I enjoyed my laborer's company much more. Andy, in turn, seemed to learn to trust that my own statements were not sarcastic. The first time I told him I appreciated his help and that he did excellent work, he asked if I was kidding. But after a while he softened up. I once told him that I trusted him not to make long-distance phone calls when I left him alone in the house. He thanked me and said he hoped he wouldn't disappoint me, as little flurries of happiness and self-doubt gusted across his face.

After he'd finished with the gutters and the shed, I had Andy paint the inside of the closets, seal the cracked plaster in the basement, stop a small leak in the drain of the tub, and install a carbon monoxide detector in the hallway. These, too, were necessary repairs and improvements I'd been putting off for some time. Around one in the afternoon, I was in the habit of giving Andy a peanut butter and jelly sandwich, carrot sticks, a plate of sugar cookies, and a glass of milk. He would say, "I can't believe I'm eating peanut butter and jelly on white bread!" as though it were some terribly exotic delicacy. When I remarked on this, he said it reminded him of the lunches he would have eaten as a child if his mother hadn't been so busy liberating animals from cancer research labs, an activity that often landed her in police lockup. When she wasn't in jail, Andy said, she was usually in the backyard hutch, where she spent the nights nursing tumorous bunnies. I found this disturbing, and when I questioned him further, he said it wasn't really that bad. He could usually find something to eat in the cupboard, like some dry oatmeal.

Then he returned to his favorite subject—a girl named Aisha who had necked with him one night after a rock performance, but didn't return his phone calls, and didn't even say hello when he ran into her in the doorway of a bar one wild night. I asked him what was so special about Aisha and he said the most special thing about her was that she had necked with him, when most other girls wouldn't.

After this I felt that I should do something for the poor boy, so while he was working on the drain, I made him a tuna casserole to take home for supper. I left it outside, on the seat of his motorcycle, wrapped in foil. The next morning, he returned the pan to my cupboard. He came in and took off his cap and accepted the espresso coffee I offered him, but I could see that something was bothering him. He began to say something, then stopped, then started again, all while stealing glances at my face as if I had some deformity he was trying not to stare at directly.

"Well, Andy," I said, "you'd better just come out with it."

After a bit of hemming and hawing, he told me that he thought the tuna casserole was delicious, and that he appreciated my thoughtfulness in making it for him, but he was concerned that I had done so out of some motherly impulse.

"What's wrong," I wanted to know, "with a motherly impulse?"

"Nothing's wrong with it," he said. "This might sound kind of weird, but actually, I think of you more as a friend."

A friend. Imagine! With an old hen like me.

———

I had Andy help me with some stepping-stones for the back yard. We made them ourselves by pouring ready-mix concrete into greased cake pans, like the *Ladies Home Journal* recommended. We banged on the side of the pans with a hammer to free them from the grip of the rectilinear forms, and I thought they came out quite nicely. They were light pink and matched the house paint. Lisa, my eldest, had informed me that pink was old-fashioned and that if I wanted to be "with it," I should paint the house terra cotta with deep purple accent trim. I told her that if she was only going to visit her old mom every three years she shouldn't give a hoot what color I painted it. Furthermore, if she had the right to tell me what color to paint my own house, then I had the right to tell her to stop bleaching her gorgeous brown hair the color of muddied hay. She replied that her hair wasn't even close to the color of muddied hay, but I wouldn't know that because I hadn't seen her new hair color yet or even her breast implants. Breast implants! I almost choked on my tea! Then she said she'd call me after the conclusion of her exercise class, but I guess it's still going on because she never did.

Andy said he liked the pink; he even remarked on how it matched the toaster. I was glad to find someone who appreciated my home, since daughters certainly don't. They only call to complain about how they're too busy to visit, and explain that they're forced to get treatments at health clubs to relieve stress. I was reminded of this one afternoon when I noticed Andy examining some dusty old greeting cards my youngest had sent. I'd grown accustomed to watching Andy's face brighten when he poked through my bric-a-brac. "Oh my God! This lamp is awesome!" he'd exclaim, gesturing with reverence at the driftwood table lamp I got in the Village in the sixties; or he'd say, "This is totally amazing!" pointing to my collection of African fertility carvings. But when he picked up those dusty old cards he looked sad, particularly hairless and beaten down, and for the first time it occurred to me that maybe Andy had nearly finished his work around the house. Maybe there wasn't much labor left to be done.

I guess I wasn't ready to give him up just yet, though, so next I had Andy arrange the stepping-stones in the yard. They led to a bare area with some dying grass where we'd once kept a birdbath. That was where I asked him to start digging. I specified the circumference of the hole but not the depth. I think I said, Why don't we just wing it on the depth?

I spent those mild spring days in the sunroom, working on my needlepoint, while Andy's shovel wheezed in the background. He got started later in the morning, which was fine with me, since the light was lasting longer and I'd been staying up later since, now and then, in the evenings, I'd meet Andy and his young friends at a nightclub and listen to his group, The Rudimentary Organs, play rock and roll. Really, it had been years since I'd been in a nightclub, or even a barroom. It seemed to me that the walls were dirtier, the music was louder, and the young people wore clothing that was far less becoming than I remembered from the old days.

Well, I had fun. The first time I attended, Andy gave me a set of plugs to wear in my ears and sat me down at a table with some of his friends, a young man named Mike and another young man, also named Mike. There were some girls, too, though not that Aisha I'd heard so much about. Flora, you know I've never been a social butterfly, but on those evenings, I felt quite amiable. There was no end to the compliments Andy's friends paid me. The girls cooed over my hats and dresses, and the boys were crazy about my old Ford. One of the Mikes even asked me what it had been like to buy leaded gas.

Andy's group made a horrible racket, but I smiled and nodded along with what passed for melody, because I knew those kids were doing the best they could, what with growing up in homes without milk in the refrigerator, or clean sheets, or even, in many cases, fathers. I knew for a fact that Andy had never had the benefit of piano lessons or even school band. When he played his electrical guitar he would take off his shirt and go bare-chested, which I suppose was a bit indulgent but I really didn't care. It's funny, what you give up caring about. Those girls would smoke cigarettes and wear stained undershirts without brassieres underneath, and when they talked they didn't make any sense, and the boys would stare out into space and make the girls pay for their bottles of beer. They were all tattooed, and not a single one of them seemed to have a last name.

"Oh," I'd say, when the music lulled, "you kids, you Generation X-ers. Anything goes with you Generation X-ers!" But really, I was just poking fun. The kids would cringe when I said "Generation X-ers." You can bet I was on to something then! "You darn Generation X ers!" I kept exclaiming.

After a few of these expeditions, I felt as though I was starting to learn a little about the state of young people today, and more than ever, they are steeped in contradictions. They seemed starved for attention and liked to tell me about their lives and backgrounds. Sometimes I just listened; sometimes I asked questions. I learned that almost all their parents got divorced when they were children and they grew up in empty houses watching a cartoon called

Scooby-Doo about a magic dog who would fulfill all their needs. Many considered themselves homosexual, though they usually slept with members of the opposite sex; none of them had ever opened a savings account or had any job training, and most had no desire for marriage or children. Objects seemed to hold a wealth of meaning for them, though they bragged of obtaining their furniture out of a trash barrel—this has a name: *Dumpster diving.* They looked dirty but bathed often, then applied creams and lotions to their hair to make it look dirty again.

I will tell you about one of these evenings, Flora, just to give you a slice of life. I remember Andy had left the table to set up some amplifiers. I had a cold, and one of the girls had given me a vitamin tablet, vitamin V, she called it. She said it cured anything. I felt especially at peace that evening. I liked watching Andy's hands as he strung cords over the stage area, the same way I liked watching him tinker around my house. The young lady kept bringing me glasses of ginger ale. She would have been pretty if she hadn't been wearing an old day dress from the 1950s, when it had been ironed last. But she was congenial and kept bending down to whisper in my ear. She'd say, "Here you go, dear," and give me a fresh napkin. I told her I wanted to know how come none of the girls wanted to go with Andy, when he was so sweet and well-behaved, and she said she didn't know but she'd ask around among the other Generation X-ers.

When Andy came down off the stage, he motioned toward a skinny little girl with black tattoos crawling up her legs. "Aisha," he whispered. He and I had continued to dis-

sect his liaisons with Aisha. There had been another incident where Aisha had led Andy out into an alley and necked
with him, recklessly. And once again, Aisha had decided she
would ignore Andy whenever she saw him.

He said he couldn't take his eyes off her, he couldn't stop
thinking about her.

"You don't need her," I pointed out.

"Are you kidding?" He had that particular hangdog look
he was in the habit of giving me, and he was blushing all the
way down to his belt, because he still hadn't put his shirt
back on. "I don't even like her. Do you think I'm a total jerk?"

Looking at that half-naked boy, I realized how relieved I
was to be young no longer. Young people have all that energy to hope for crazy things that cause them harm, and I
can't imagine anything more miserable than loneliness
tarted up as hope. Loneliness—that beast! I told Andy so. I
told him that hope is a winged dragon guarding a beautiful
golden urn. And inside the urn is the ilk of Aisha.

Andy sniffed my glass and tried to give me a ride home,
but Flora, you know I haven't touched the stuff in years.

I kept Andy busy digging in the yard. After a week or two,
the hole was three or four feet deep with the circumference
of a kiddy pool. Andy shoveled slowly, which was fine. I'd go
visit him out there in the afternoons, after we'd lunched, to
inspect his work. "Is it just a hole," Andy asked, "or are you
going to want to put something in it?"

"It's just a hole," I told him.

Andy stopped his work and leaned on his shovel. He'd look me in the eye briefly and then look away for a long time—some days he seemed especially shy. He would ask me questions: "Do you want me to put the rocks by the fence?" Or "Are we still winging it on depth?"

Yes, I told him, we were. We were both quite satisfied with it, I think. It was good work. Occasionally a neighbor would stop by to see what kind of progress Andy had made. Everybody agreed that it was shaping up into a fine pit.

The days were getting hotter so Andy would often come in for a break in the afternoon. I'd make some sun tea or else lemonade from a can of frozen concentrate garnished with slices of real lemon. I learned that there was another young lady batting her eyes at Andy, a girl named Pauline, who had once had anorexia nervosa, which as you probably know is an ailment that strikes girls on diets. I suggested that Andy bring her some of my sugar cookies and he said, "Actually, that might freak her out." He sipped his lemonade and sprawled his long legs across the kitchen floor. He was wearing his cap in the house, and rather than being offended I felt pleased—that we had become so comfortable together he had forgotten to take it off.

Aisha, meanwhile, had come alive when she realized this Pauline was sweet on Andy.

"She keeps walking up to me and touching my chest," Andy protested. "She puts her hand on my chest while she talks to me. Is this normal?"

I told him that normal varied from culture to culture and time to time. Once it had been normal for people to live their lives according to visions they saw in their dreams.

"I can't even pay attention to what she's saying," he said. "It's like I blank out when she's touching my chest. It's weird."

"In my day, people danced," I said. "They touched each other in a lot of places then."

A few days later he told me that Pauline had become angry, because he was spotted kissing Aisha again, and now neither one would talk to him. The two girls, though, had become fast friends—bonding on their mutual interest in ignoring poor Andy. They began doing their hair the same way, in little pigtails (symbolizing, perhaps, a presexual state). "I'm so pathetic," Andy said. I watched him curling over, as though someone had punched him in the stomach, or as though he was trying to make himself small, with a pain that seemed almost physical.

"Maybe you could get *into* being pathetic," I suggested. "Maybe you'd like that."

He gave me a wide-eyed look.

I lit up one of Andy's clove cigarettes. I thought I'd just give it a try. What the hell.

―――――

We finally had one of our warm summer rains. I went outside just after dawn in my robe and galoshes. Andy had been working hard and the hole was quite deep. The sides had sloshed in on themselves and the bottom resembled a big tub of chocolate milk. A few earthworms that hadn't made it floated in the water. The whole yard was luminous in the dawn light—everything was glazed and shiny and somehow endless. The changes weather brings have never ceased to amaze me, Flora. How is it that a little rainstorm could make my own backyard look so radiant? Even the pit looked lovely, with its dark glow. It occurred to me how much better it was that way. It was better to have a pit in the backyard than to have it inside myself.

I stood there for a while and thought about all the sad life stories I'd been collecting from Andy and the other young people I'd been associating with. I thought about the little girls from broken homes whose fathers had run off with Danish au pairs; I thought about the boys raised in hippie camps with parents who told them that flush toilets were the work of capitalist pigs. I thought of poor Andy, with his mother so hell-bent on saving rabbits and greyhounds and three-legged cats that she forgot to take care of her own son. There were other stories too, ones that I found just a bit too familiar for comfort. A few of the girls complained to me about their mothers, overbearing women who seemed com- pelled to tell them how to comb their hair and button their shirts and chew their food. These mothers were full of warnings. Only tarts and chippies lightened their hair, they said, or wore athletic shorts, or pierced their ears, or walked around with their nail polish peeling off. I stood in the yard, looking at the dark glow, thinking about how I'd done those things too. I'd been too exacting: I'd pushed my girls away. I'd changed love into something difficult when it ought to have been the easiest thing in the world. Oh, Flora. How do you dig a pit that can contain all of that?

———

Andy showed up later that morning, though given the wet weather I think it was obvious to both of us that he wouldn't be doing any digging in the yard. He was soaked from riding his motorcycle over from the house where he lived with some other young people and a bunch of cats that kept having kittens nobody wanted to take care of. There had been dirty dishes that sat in the sink for so long, he told me, that his housemates finally gave up and threw them in the trash.

When I opened the door, he was wiping his boots on the mat. "I didn't think you'd have any work for me," he said, "but I thought I'd come over anyway to see if you wanted some company."

He kept wiping his boots as if he couldn't bear to meet my eye. Sometimes that boy looked so sad. I wondered if he'd have been happier if he'd had more hair. Maybe if things had gone differently for him, if his parents had fed him iron tablets, or sent him to one of those Danish preschools where all the toys are made of wood, he would have kept his hair with him a little longer. Maybe he would have had a little more fuel to survive on when times were tough. Young people today, it seems to me, are sadder than they used to be.

We sat at the kitchen table and drank espresso. His shirt was wet, so I put him in one of Hank's old ones, with the collar and cuffs. Andy didn't look so much the boy in my husband's shirt. He looked like a young man. He started to tell me about Aisha; she'd been at it again. She'd come by in the middle of the night and left him a passionate note, but when he called her on the telephone she sobbed and said that she was moving to France. Andy hung his head in despair.

After that we listened to the radio playing for a while, just sitting quietly with the radio and the rain falling on the roof, and then Andy asked if I'd teach him how to dance.

I said that I would, if I could remember myself. We stood where that ugly yellow linoleum had been (there'd been a hardwood floor underneath it all the time), and I did my best to teach Andy an easy waltz. He wasn't very good at it, and to tell the truth, neither was I, but I think that what we were doing still qualified as dancing.

"I was looking at the hole this morning," I said. "You did a good job with that."

"Really? Are you sure?"

I told him that I was. I told him that this was about all the hole I needed at this point.

"As soon as the dirt dries," I said, "I want you to come over and start filling it in."

It was Frank Sinatra singing on the radio. Flora, would you ever have thought I'd be dancing in the kitchen at this point in my life, in the middle of the morning, with a handsome young man? Andy couldn't stop stepping on my toes. But that didn't make it any less sweet.

Yours truly,
Virginia

DUET

13

The girls were thirteen when they met on the first Saturday of the school year, in the Pre-College program, at Juilliard. It was a heady ending to a terrible day because up until then, Clara's experience at conservatory had been a disaster. She'd started with high hopes, certain she'd spend the day immersed in the best of Western culture. Of course she would, it was Juilliard! Where intellectual adventures awaited! She would meet gray-haired teachers with sonorous voices, who would wander into the classroom still clutching great books. She would be surrounded by the heady, architectural presence of Lincoln Center, with its travertine halls—Lincoln Center! Where the work of great performers had been celebrated since 1968 (according to her father)! And she'd make friends with all the other children, children who would be just like her—in love with classical music, eighteenth-century Europe, and the sound of their instruments. They too would be prone to tripping around in a fog, practicing fingerings in the air. It would be completely different from regular school. This time, Clara would not be the little priss with the cello.

By the end of the day, she'd endured a festival of disillusionment. She'd been hauling her cello through the warren of halls since nine in the morning because she couldn't find her locker. They were not travertine halls. They were carpeted and musty smelling due to the amazing fact that not a single window in the entire building opened. No one had spoken to her (except her teacher), and after a while Clara began to hunch her shoulders in an effort to shield herself from the other students, who all seemed more confident and sophisticated than she was. The girl violin players were particularly imposing. They reminded her of ballerinas or racehorses, revved up and high-strung, galloping through the halls. The red marks throbbing on their necks identified them as members of an exclusive club, one that didn't include Clara.

By the last class of the day Clara was utterly dispirited, though the usual refrain was still whisking through her head like a metronome: *everything's great, everything's great, everything's great*. Nevertheless, she dragged her cello to the back of the solfège room and slumped in a chair. It did, at least, seem unlikely that things could get any worse. She'd almost cried during her lesson but managed to control herself. When Clara entered the room, her teacher had said, "Now is your turn, sweet-hard," in a Russian accent. Everyone raved about Miss Vlanofsky—such a wonderful teacher! (though not as good as Mrs. Westmoreland, according to her father)—so Clara was shocked (shocked!) when, as she was running through scales, her teacher pulled out a cardboard canister and began inserting potato chips into her mouth.

Clara tried to ignore this and played a Brahms sonata she'd known for years. When she finished, she smiled in anticipation. Her teachers always praised her playing on this particular piece.

But Miss Vlanofsky rolled her eyes. "God in heaven, what are you thinking? This is music, not snapping together dominoes! Flow! Flow! Make it flow!"

"I don't understand," said Clara. "Aren't the notes right?"

Miss Vlanofsky leaned forward. "Yes. The notes are right. They are *exactly* right."

Clara played the Brahms again. Before she'd finished, Miss Vlanofsky sprang from her chair and ran out of the room. When she returned, she was holding a jar filled with a clear, viscous fluid. She sighed dramatically as she sat down and began to work it into her flushed cheeks.

"Aloe vera gel," she said.

Clara looked at her face. It was bright red.

"You will learn," Miss Vlanofsky said. It sounded like a threat.

So it was with relief and amazement that she watched Jo walk across the room and collapse into the chair beside her. Jo Eberdell! Jo was such a good violin player that Clara had heard of her before even stepping a foot inside Juilliard. She had a reputation as a prodigy, a budding superstar, a natural on the violin who *never practiced*. Rumor had it that after school she went home and played Nintendo. Clara, by contrast, practiced for four hours a day. She'd never seen a Nintendo system. The kids at her school liked to tease her by making jokes involving *The Simpsons*. She'd never seen *The Simpsons*. Of course she knew about it—"a humorous cartoon family." She wasn't a total dork.

Jo leaned forward and looked right at Clara. She was pretty, taller than the other Asian and part-Asian girls, with long, swingy hair that seemed to lag a few seconds behind the rest of her.

"Do you bleach your hair?" she said.

"What?" said Clara.

"Well, your hair has such nice highlights I just wondered if you bleached it."

"Oh no. I would never be allowed to do something like that."

Jo huffed and rolled her eyes. "That figures. What else aren't you allowed to do?"

Clara paused—she could never tell when people were making fun of her. "Drink more than one Coke," she finally said. "Watch channels other than PBS. Get anything less than an A. Shave my legs."

"No way! You still can't shave your legs!" Jo cupped her hand over her mouth and giggled. Something emanated from her—a crackle in the air, a sharpness in her eyes— Clara thought it might be intelligence, or charm, or both.

She was hit by a jolt of exhilaration, and her upper lip broke out in a sweat.

"Can I see?" asked Jo.

Clara felt shy but she bent down anyway and pulled up her pants leg. Jo leaned over and stroked her furry shin.

"Wow. And you're a teenager! That's outrageous." She was laughing—pleased, so pleased—Clara was delighted. At least she hadn't spent her first day at Juilliard disappointing everyone. "Okay, now I'm totally convinced that my theory is correct. Classical musicians are the most sheltered kids in the world! Am I right?"

Clara nodded solemnly. She'd never thought of herself as sheltered—more like protected. But with a word, Jo had punched a hole through a wall and let the air rush in.

"Is there anything else you can't do?"

Clara chewed on her cheek. There *was* something. She'd never told anyone. She leaned forward and whispered, "I'm not supposed to ride the subway."

Jo gasped. "What? You mean you've *never* ridden the subway?"

"No."

"Why not?"

Clara gave it some thought. "Because it's too dangerous?" she tried.

"Oh my God. It's not dangerous. It's fun! Let's go."

"Now? Are you kidding? We have solfège."

"Ugh, please. I hate it. It's useless, *Sound of Music* crap. Let's ditch."

"Oh no, I can't. Thank you very much for the invitation, but I can't. I have my cello." Clara felt her hands go damp. Missing class was entirely out of the question. She would die. Her head would explode. But first her parents would die while expressing their disappointment in English, German, and French. As they were dying, they'd remind Clara how hard her grandparents had worked to escape the old country, and with their last breaths they'd croak, *What would the rabbi say?*

Jo's eyes hardened. Her bangs swung down, framing her gray eyes so they looked like chunks of granite. She started her bombardment: "Do you want to miss everything normal people do? Won't your music suffer if you don't experience regular things? Don't you ever want to have an adventure?" Her cheeks flushed and the red mark on her neck darkened. She looked amazing; she looked like a creature who had just broken free from a marauding strangler.

Clara folded her hands in her lap. "I can't," she said. "I'm sorry, but there's simply no way."

Jo took a breath and continued. "Don't you think Yo-Yo Ma takes public transportation? Do you want to be a Goody Two-shoes for the rest of your life? Do you want to be thirty years old and never have been on the subway?"

"But I have my cello."

"So bring it."

In the end, Clara didn't even make a decision. She was pulled out of her chair—sucked, really—and out of the building toward the 66th Street station. There were times later on when she wondered: if Jo hadn't had those dimples,

if she hadn't already been renowned, and if she hadn't ignored everyone else in the class and chosen Clara, what
would her life have been like? Flat, boring, and gray. But at
the time, she was only thinking about how her father's face
would look if they were caught. They jogged through the
intersection and toward the subway entrance—it was dirty,
incredibly dirty. Clara paused at the top, panting, slightly off
balance; she had the sensation that she was about to topple
down the stairwell. A blast of hot air rushed up to meet her,
carrying the smell of urine, metal, darkness, and speed.

Jo turned, laughing, and grabbed her by the hand. Clara
plunged down the stairs after her and the sky disappeared.
Giddiness swept over her—she felt as though everything inside her were bursting open—as though she were ripping off
her clothes, eating dirt, swearing, not practicing, stomping
her feet at the dinner table, and going to bed without brushing her teeth.

Oh, she was wild now.

The next Saturday, Clara was allowed to visit Jo's apartment after class. To her great surprise, no one had informed Clara's parents that she had missed solfège. The
idea that she might be able to get away with things was
new to her, and a little unsettling. Still, Clara was desperate to be Jo's friend and so had sworn to several things
about which she had no firsthand knowledge: she told her
mother that they would walk directly to Jo's building from
campus. When they arrived, there would be responsible

adult supervision; she would avoid eating teeth-rotting snacks made of pure sugar.

"Maybe you girls could work on some music," suggested her mother, a little starstruck, as was Clara, when she learned that Jo had already—at twelve!—served as concertmaster of the Juilliard Pre-College Orchestra. Clara herself was still only in Symphony, which wasn't nearly as good. But once they got to Jo's apartment, it became clear that they weren't going to work on music; instead, they consumed Twinkies while sprawling on the floor watching reruns of a famous television show that Clara had never heard of. There were pictures of Jo's parents on the piano—a pretty Asian woman and an owlish Caucasian man. Jo was already towering over both of them, shot up on American milk. But there were no actual parents in the apartment.

Though Jo's apartment wasn't much bigger than their own, it had a lot more windows, and Clara suspected that her mother would call it elegant. Jo gave her a tour of the bedrooms and the gigantic kitchen. Contrary to the rumors, the apartment contained abundant evidence that Jo practiced her instrument. A music stand was set up in her room beside the pink desk chair ("my mother likes things really girly"), and her parts were spread across the bed. Of course, the best evidence had been in front of Clara all along—the red mark on Jo's neck. A person had to log a lot of hours with a violin crammed under her chin to get one of those calluses, if that was the right word, though it wasn't as hard as a callus. (Jo's seemed to be oozing—she had a bandage over it.) Clara had a mark of her own under her clothes where her cello hit her chest, right over her heart. She had all sorts of sentimental feelings about this mark but was pretty sure that Jo would think they were corny, the way she thought that Eugene Johnson's piano-key scarf was corny. She was learning a lot from Jo.

"Let's paint our toenails," suggested Jo.

Clara tilted her head in puzzlement. "Really?"

Jo laughed. "You never have, right?"

"No. Isn't it sort of . . . trashy?"

Jo laughed harder, covering her mouth with her hand, with tears starting to trickle down the side of her face. Though Jo was technically laughing *at* her, there was something about the exchange that felt delightful. It felt as if she were giving Jo her innocence, dropping it at her feet like a bone. Maybe Jo was going to take it away somewhere and bury it.

That afternoon Clara assimilated the preliminary facts about pedicures in front of the TV. Then Jo took her into the bathroom and taught her about makeup. "Tasteful makeup," she emphasized. Clara ended up with lip gloss and powder and a little mascara, smeared from fits of hysterical laughing that gripped them in waves. Clara looked slightly older when she was made up, just enough to nudge her over the line from girl to young woman. When they were done with that, Jo showed her how to squeeze blackheads with tissue-wrapped fingers; Clara found this activity fascinating and strangely intimate, like telling secrets.

"I wish I had a sister," Clara said, and blushed. What she really meant was that she wished Jo was her sister, but she was learning that it was what a person didn't say that kept her from being a loser.

They spent the remainder of the afternoon consuming a can of Duncan Hines frosting and watching cartoons. No adults ever materialized. Much later, Clara learned that Jo's mother had already returned to Japan—on a temporary but never-ending basis—to resume her career as a translator. Her father worked as some sort of business executive. Most of the time, Jo was watched by her aunt.

When Clara's mother rang the bell, the frosting can was lying on the floor and Clara was smeared with Maybelline products. Clara took one look at her mother's face and with no preparation whatsoever began what was to become a life-long strategy for dealing with her parents' impossible demands: lying.

"Jo's mom just went downstairs to pick up the mail," she said. Clara's mother walked into the living room. "Jo's brother was making a cake." Clara's mother seemed not to hear her. As she walked around the apartment clutching her pocketbook, she kept turning to Clara and saying, *See?* "See Jo's shelf full of scores?" She pointed, as though Clara didn't have scores of her own. "Isn't that impressive? See?" she gestured toward a certificate Jo had won in a violin competition. "Look at this room," she exclaimed, sweeping her hand toward several half-destroyed cubes of rosin and the pile of music strewn across Jo's bedspread. She made the whole circuit again, going from room to room, pointing out evidence of Jo's accomplishments as though Clara were a lazy slugabed in need of correction rather what she was: the most compliant little girl in the world.

16

At sixteen, Clara judged herself to be objectively pretty but not at all attractive. Her frizzy hair and shuffling walk eclipsed her good features: big eyes, straight teeth, and what her grandmother referred to as "a nice figure" (i.e., a C-cup). Jo would occasionally try to prop her up but she did it without enthusiasm, as though she secretly believed that Clara was essentially a creature devoid of charisma. Jo, on the other hand, had become a lit-up beauty, sweet-faced and willowy, with hair so shiny and dark that Clara had actually seen it reflect neon signs. Jo had taken it upon herself to coach Clara in the womanly arts of flirting and self-display, but it was an uphill climb. The girls had already spent half the afternoon wandering around the Village, with Jo trailing Clara and whispering, "Smile at him! Him!" Clara, meanwhile, continued to walk in her customary manner, with her eyes downcast, examining the many, many pieces of gum ground into hard, black disks on the sidewalk.

Clara was still shy, painfully shy. Boys filled her with giddy terror. The NYU college boys were the worst; they were adorable, so frightening that she couldn't even look at them, but Jo was helping her overcome her fear. After a block, Jo stopped. "This isn't working."

"I can't do it," said Clara. "I can't look them in the eye. I can't smile. What if they kiss me?"

"Kiss you? Why? You're just walking down the street."

"What if they tell me I'm fat and stupid and ugly and talentless?"

"Clara, you're freaking out. The main thing is to *look*, open your eyes, don't walk around with your eyes lowered! Be present! It's not for their benefit, anyway, it's for you. You don't have to smile. You could just scowl at them instead."

"Scowl? Like a mean person?"

"Why not? It's a start."

It seemed worth a shot. Clara tried again, strolling down Bleeker Street with Jo in her wake, scowling at cute boys, medium boys, and not-so-cute boys. They grinned back; they turned their heads to watch her go; they ignored her; they raised their eyebrows in surprise. She kept her head up for the whole length of the block—it was unbelievable! Jo's plan was brilliant. Why hadn't she learned this herself from all the years of lessons and parental wheedling? Disapproval was far more powerful than kindness. At the end of the block, she ducked into a doorway; Jo crowded after her and lit a cigarette. They took turns puffing on it until a bag lady on the steps began cursing at them and they tumbled back onto the sidewalk and headed toward the park.

"I once asked my dad why people had to sleep on the street," Clara still loved giving Jo these gifts, the stories of her long and arduous dorkhood, "and he said it was because they didn't practice their instruments."

Jo doubled over laughing—she was so pretty that half the people on the sidewalk turned to look at her. "That's so sick. Did you believe him?"

"Of course!" Clara kept a straight face. "I always believe my dad."

Jo took Clara's arm and tipped her chin at a pensive angle. "There is something intriguing to that. I mean, wouldn't it be interesting if everybody really did play an instrument?" Jo gestured at the other people lurking in the park. "Can you imagine? What if classical music was part of people's lives, instead of just something they listened to when they were stressed-out in traffic?"

"You mean, it's not?"

Jo stopped and turned to Clara. "You're kidding, right?"

"No, I mean, of course I know everyone doesn't play the cello, but people must at least sort of think . . . that Beethoven is great? That Haydn's string quartets—" she paused, seeing the look on Jo's face, but made herself go on—"are sublime?"

Jo had a funny look—half pained, half amused. "Uh-oh. No, honey. I hate to be the one to break it to you, but probably most of these people, if not all of them, have never thought about Haydn's string quartets, ever. Not even once."

Clara took a breath and started to say something, but when she saw the fierceness on Jo's face she stopped.

Jo leaned forward—her expression was intense, verging on mean. "We've spent our whole lives trying to perfect something most people don't give a shit about. In fact, they don't even *think* about it."

Clara took a step backward and bumped into someone. She felt tears building up behind her eyes. "No."

"Yes."

"You're exaggerating. It can't be that bad!"

"Don't cry. Oh my God, you've got to get out more. We're freaks, Clara. We're trained monkeys. I thought you knew."

Clara wiped her eyes and started walking. "I do know, I just don't believe it the way you do. Maybe some of these people will discover music later in life, or something. Maybe it will bring them great joy."

Jo raised a brow. "You can believe that if you want. I just don't want you to turn into a person who doesn't use her brain."

"I'm using it," Clara forced a smile and squeezed her friend's arm. "I'm just using it optimistically."

Later that afternoon, they went back to Clara's apartment and sprawled on her bed, listening to the Ravel Duo for violin and cello on her stereo. Her mother knocked on the door every ten minutes, bringing them bagels and lox and cucumber salad until Clara burst out, "Leave us alone!" and Jo cackled with such pure amusement that Clara's mom was infected and started laughing herself.

"You silly girls," she said, and left.

When the music was over, Clara rolled onto her stomach. "My teacher keeps telling me to play from my vagina."

"No way. What exactly does she say?"

"'Play from your vagina, my dear.'"

"Wow. You should get that on tape. We'll put it in the crazy-teacher archive."

"What does Miss Watson say?" Clara felt timid even saying her name—Jo's teacher was so painfully famous, so renowned for turning out world-class soloists.

"'Now, my little sugar plum, you mustn't disparage the Wieniawski—it will wow the jury.' I just blow her off."

"You do? You blow off Julia Watson?" Clara couldn't believe it; it was as though she had said, I piss on the Torah.

Jo laughed. "I just don't always agree with her, that's all."

Clara blinked. This fact stunned her into silence. She shoved a piece of a bagel into her mouth and chewed it while her mind drifted. "Do you think I'll ever have a boyfriend?" she finally said.

"Why, do you like someone?"

Clara blushed. "I can't say. I'm too embarrassed. If I say it I'll die."

"You know you want to tell me."

"Don't tease me, okay? You have to promise never to say anything, ever. Not to me, not to anyone, ever again. I can't stand it. I'm thoroughly mortified."

Jo shoved a piece of herring in her mouth. "I promise."

"I sort of think I like Marshall Uppgaard."

"The flute player?"

"Uh-huh."

Jo chewed with her mouth open. "Interesting."

"Do you think he's lame?" Clara's voice trembled. "Is there something kind of off about him? Is the flute too gay?"

"God, I don't know. I don't even know him," Jo said, "but if you like him, I'm sure he's cool."

"What should I do? Do you think I should scowl at him?"

"Absolutely." Jo shot her a sweet, dimpled smile. She gripped Clara's arm. "You know what?" Jo said. "We'll always be friends."

Much later, Clara mused that Jo had given her the run of her own mind. Clara thought of her teenage self as a stump of wood, a follower, and a deadly boring cellist, but Jo snapped her out of it. Jo inhabited music the way a fish lived in water—it was her world to explore. She was always making connections, hearing nuances, finding metaphors; she had the confidence to wonder about things that Clara thought were etched in stone, like the sanctity of Miss Watson's teaching.

But the biggest revelation was the way she played the violin. Even at sixteen, she'd begun to develop a style that wrenched Clara's heart—Jo always held something back, just a little; it suggested a well of deep feeling running beneath the music. Her sound was clear and loud (all of Miss Watson's students were loud), but her playing was restrained, a balance of emotion and intellect. Jo even looked different from other violinists when she played: most had a sort of standard concerto expression—eyes closed, jaw loose, brows raised—but Jo stared straight ahead, vaguely tough, and smiled when a phrase pleased her. The audience was entranced. So was Clara.

Yet there was this: three weeks after Clara confessed her crush on Marshall Uppgaard, she turned the corner in the Juilliard library and found Jo standing on her toes, kissing him in the choral music section. The two of them dated for the rest of high school.

"I can't believe you did that," Clara said, trying to push down her hurt.

Jo turned to her with a blank stare. "Did what?"

Clara didn't say anything else.

24

After seven years of Juilliard—undergraduate and most of graduate school—Clara was finally getting out of New York. She'd been awarded a Fulbright to study in Berlin, and for her last night in town, she and Jo had planned an evening of mild debauchery. First, Jo would play her recital (one of many), then they'd knock back martinis in O'Neal's until closing time. The goal was to stay up all night since Clara had to catch a cab to the airport at 5 A.M., anyway. Clara felt a thrum of happiness at the prospect of spending an evening with her friend. Jo was too busy for her a lot of the time now. Ever since she'd won the Indianapolis violin competition (astounding!) their paths had diverged. Jo was always traveling to concerts, hanging out with conductors, shopping for gowns; she'd taken out a loan and bought herself a beautiful Amati violin. Clara's life, on the other hand, was pretty much the same at ever: she was studying at Juilliard, buying her clothes at the Gap, and living at home.

Though now there was a hand-lettered sign on the door to her room. It said *Knock Before Entering.*

Clara shuffled down the aisle to a back-row seat. She sat with her shoulders hunched, chewing on the inside of her cheek while Jo played an angular Bartók sonata. Something had gone wrong with the air-conditioning and the auditorium was stifling; between movements, a fluttering rose from the audience as people fanned their faces with their programs. Still, Clara had no trouble concentrating on the music. She marveled, as usual, at Jo's playing—such intelligence and restraint, such rhythmic freedom. Though Bartók was not quite her style, personally. Clara still loved the Romantic era best; she played with all the warmth she could muster, then went home and hugged her cat until he squealed.

After the concert, Clara leaned against a stack of folding chairs while Jo greeted audience members in the green room. "Here come the daughter groupies," Jo whispered, as elderly couples tottered toward her. They shook her hand and praised her playing—they all seemed knocked out by Jo's youth. Jo smiled and chatted, perfectly poised, but during a lull she towed Clara into a quiet corner. "I wish they'd just come out and say what they're really thinking: 'Such a nice girl,'" Jo said, "'such a hardworking Japanese girl, unlike my ungrateful wretch of a child, who never calls.'"

Clara laughed, pleasantly shocked by Jo's habit—perhaps a bit cynical—of cutting through the flourishes to the core of things. Jo was on a sort of rampage that night, criticizing the audience, criticizing other players, and haranguing their friends. She was seeping bitterness. "You're all so obnoxious," she said, sipping a martini at the bar later, "truly obnoxious." She'd pushed her chair back from a table full of their fellow musicians. A series of jokes dealing with the color, weight, and texture of various player's bowel movements had started to wind through the group. "What is it with classical musicians and fourth-grade humor?" Jo wanted to know. "You're all perfect children in fossilized form—always pleasing your parents, pleasing your teachers, sucking up to the audience. But get a couple of drinks into you, and you turn into naughty kids making bathroom jokes. It's pathetic."

They all stared at her for a moment before Anton Lee (the great piano player) turned around and launched into a constipation saga.

But Clara (who'd been laughing herself) turned her chair toward Jo. "Okay," she said, "you might have a point, but I'm not sure you can make such sweeping generalizations. I'm sure plenty of classical musicians are very grown-up and dignified and all that."

"I see obedient children in adult bodies. What's the point in thinking independently? It's never rewarded."

"No! It's always rewarded. Jo! Look at you—it's been rewarded in you! I really don't think it's that bad."

"Come on. What do you know?" said Jo. Her eyelids were heavy and her lips were pulled back in a sneer. "You still have a pile of stuffed animals on your bed."

Clara felt tears spring to her eyes—her lack of sophistication had always delighted Jo. Now she felt childish and stupid. "I just think they have a right to blow off steam," she said softly. "I just don't think everything is so fundamentally screwed up."

Jo tapped a cocktail skewer against her teeth. "You'd never admit it if it was."

That might be true, she probably wouldn't admit it, but Clara didn't want to dwell on it. Was there something so wrong with the bright side? "Can we please not fight?" she said. "I'm leaving in a few hours."

27

When she came back from Europe, Clara called Jo every day. She memorized every nuance of her outgoing message but Jo never called back. For a week or two Clara ignored the rumors and chalked it up to modern busy life, but after a while she arrived at the inevitable, nauseating conclusion: her best friend was avoiding her.

Clara paced around her parents' apartment, biting her nails. Her calling pattern was getting a little stalkerish, but she was afraid that Jo was sliding out of her life. While she was in Berlin, Clara had heard shocking things through the grapevine. The most disturbing was that Jo had flat-out quit performing; of course, she hadn't believed it. Why would Jo quit when things were going so well for her? Besides, just because Jo had always complained about classical music didn't mean that she didn't really love it, deep down.

So Clara decided to do what she always did when something didn't make sense to her: she set her mind in neutral and kept plugging away—usually, it was practicing, though in this case it was dialing the phone. Finally, one late afternoon, Jo picked up.

Clara's voice wavered. "What's going on? Are you mad at me? Did I do something wrong?"

"No, Clara," Jo sighed, "you've never done anything wrong in your entire life."

Jo went on to explain that she'd been very, very busy. She said she'd tell Clara all about it, and they made a hurried plan to meet. The next day, Clara slumped in one of the hundreds of Starbucks in Manhattan, kicking her feet through crumpled napkins and coffee-cup sleeves.

"I think I was in the wrong Starbucks," Clara said into Jo's machine. She thought she might as well try to provide her with a plausible excuse; it was better than thinking of her as a jerk, though only marginally.

After that, everything in New York began to seem sad—the concrete slab of Lincoln Center, where Jo had first introduced her to the concept of class-ditching, the subways she'd taught her to ride, the hot dog vendors who were in fact not selling rancid dog meat, Jo once explained, contrary to her father's admonitions. Clara kept rewinding her memories, trying to figure out what she'd done wrong. Yes, they'd fallen out of touch while she was in Europe; coordinating their schedules and the time difference had been so daunting that after a year or so, their calls slowed to a trickle. But that had been mutual—she couldn't be pissed about that? Clara had also extended her stay in Europe by several years, though she remembered how Jo had laughed and told her to enjoy every minute.

There was another possibility, but Clara hated to consider it. It seemed possible that Jo might be mad because she'd done so well lately. Jo was the better player—Jo would always be the better player!—but Clara had finally become really good herself. Something had finally clicked and she'd started to enjoy her studies. Tasks that had seemed like chores became interesting; she actually began to understand what her teacher meant when she told her to play from her vagina (though Clara, always a little prim, preferred to think of it as her second chakra—the seat of sexuality and gracefulness).

She'd begun to be recognized as an exceptional player, though it seemed that her losing twenty-five pounds (she could only stomach so much sausage and cabbage) was what finally jump-started her solo career—confirming Jo's cynicism, which Clara had always dismissed as overblown. Clara liked to think it was all about merit and hard work, but the truth was that pretty girls sold tickets. Pretty girls made for stunning entrances in strapless gowns; pretty girls looked up at the conductor with a twinge of fear, praying that his elevated spot on the podium did not give him a view down her top.

Clara knew she could never really rival Jo, but maybe— she'd dream about this as she spent the mornings practicing in Berlin—they could play a piece together. She had a vision of the two of them in Carnegie Hall, in matching gowns, playing the Ravel Duo. It was retarded, it was juvenile, Jo would laugh and tell her how corny it was.

But maybe they'd do it, anyway.

At last, when Clara was sure it was a lost cause, Jo appeared unannounced at one of Clara's performances with the New Jersey Symphony. Clara was completely taken by surprise when she showed up backstage. Jo looked different; her hair was short and she was wearing high heels and a long coat. She looked elegant and wealthy and so transformed from the Jo she remembered that she seemed as remote as a photograph. Her cheeks were flushed and Clara wondered for a second if she might be tipsy, but that thought passed as a wave of happiness flooded her. It was Jo; there could only be one.

Jo beamed. "That was wonderful." She gave Clara a hug. She was so pretty—she smelled like mints and gardenias. Her eyes glowed; she seemed genuinely proud of Clara. "That was wonderful playing. You're a wonderful girl. It's all so fucking fabulous."

Clara thought she might burst into tears. "I'm so glad to see you!"

Jo put an arm around her shoulder. "Me too."

"You'll come out to dinner with us, won't you?"

"I'd love to, but I have people waiting for me." Jo was already backing up, heading for the stage door.

"Really?" said Clara, "you're leaving?"

"It's okay," Jo said, making a phone gesture with her hand, "call me. We'll catch up."

Clara stayed in town for two more months; she tried Jo over and over, but Jo never returned her calls. When they finally happened to walk past each other one day in Penn

Station, Clara ran after her like a puppy calling, "Jo, Jo, how's it going?"

Jo stopped and gave her a flat stare. Clara assumed that she hadn't recognized her and pulled off her winter hat. Jo shoved her hands in her pockets, squinted at her for a minute and said, "Oh. Hi." Then she turned and walked away.

34

Clara had a three-night engagement, but she was staying in New York all week (in a hotel—she no longer stayed with her parents). Despite the acoustics, Clara liked playing Avery Fisher Hall and she loved playing with the Phil. Her first teacher was in the cello section, and friends from Juilliard were scattered through the orchestra. Still, even under such happy circumstances, the ridiculousness of being a classical musician hit her, on average, every other day. During rehearsals, she spotted orchestra members with magazines propped open on their stands, or wearing the scorned piano-key scarves, or brandishing mugs photo-printed with pictures of their little dogs named Bimberl or Scherzo or Allegro. Jo was right. It was a silly, regressive world where the parent-child relationship was recreated over and over—stand after stand of middle-aged players busy rebelling or else struggling to be good girls and boys—for teachers, conductors, for audiences, for nobody.

Maybe there was a bit of the obedient child still lurking in Clara, too. Her mother had never stopped comparing her to Jo—though now instead of pushing her daughter to play like her, she urged her to follow Jo's lead and "marry a rich man." Apparently, her mother had recently run into Jo on the sidewalk in front of D'Agostino. Jo gushed about the co-op she and her husband had just bought: wouldn't Mrs. Goldman stop by for their housewarming party? She could bring Clara; sure, why not.

Clara made a list of her objections: she had to play with the Phil that night and would have to either carry her dress in a garment bag or drop it off at the hall; she couldn't carry her cello and her dress both. Besides, it was too weird and she didn't want to get upset before she performed. Clara's mother cajoled; she offered to drop her things at the hall; she complained of her arthritis. Clara finally agreed, partly to placate her mother and partly out of her own curiosity. She honestly wanted to see Jo. A sanitized vision of reunion kept popping up in her head: Jo would be so happy to see her! By golly! Clara recognized the same stupid part of herself that had excused the rancor in Jo since the first day they met. But she went anyway.

The apartment was lovely, larger than she'd expected, with spotlighted corners of disarray that had to be the work of a decorator. Her mother led her from place to place saying, *See?* "See the stainless steel dishwasher? See the Persian carpets?" Clara shoved an olive in her mouth and rolled her eyes. When Jo appeared, striding across one of the Persian carpets, she was smartly dressed and as lovely as ever, though Clara found it hard to process the fact that the mark on her neck was gone. Clara's mother had already fed her pertinent bits of biographical information: Jo had taken a job in banking, she'd married another banker, she was rarely glimpsed, certainly not at concerts. When Jo said hello she was polite but distant. She introduced Clara to her husband as "Sharon's daughter, my childhood playmate," then drifted off to the stainless steel kitchen, where she started rearranging flowers. Clara found herself stuck in a corner with Jo's husband. He was handsome in a Southern way, tall but a little fat, and aggressively nice.

"Jo tells me you're a cello player!"

"That's right." She leaned away. The husband was a close-stander, but maybe he couldn't help it; some bouncy song was blasting on the stereo.

"I bet you play with the Symphony!"

"Well, not exactly. I perform with different orchestras. I'm a soloist."

He nodded and rattled the ice in his drink. He had nice shoes, a nice smile. He seemed like a very nice man. "You play all by yourself? Like they do in Neiman Marcus?"

Clara stared—she prayed that he was kidding. Jo wouldn't marry someone who knew *nothing* about music. She wouldn't wall off that part of her life entirely: all that study, the work, the music itself—it had to have meant something to her, didn't it? Of course it did. She looked at his grin; somehow he managed to be friendly without really paying attention to her. But he didn't seem to be kidding.

"Doesn't Jo ever play the violin for you?" Clara asked.

"Nah. I wouldn't mind it though. She tells me she was really something when she was a kid—the Juilliard School and all that. I was thinking of getting her a violin for her birthday."

Clara couldn't keep the expression of shock off her face. "What are you saying? She got rid of the Amati? She sold it?"

"I guess so." Her husband leaned forward. "You're a musician. Let me ask you a question: how much would a nice violin cost? Just something for Jo to get her moves back."

Clara sighed. She didn't mean to shock him but instruments were expensive. The Amati could have paid for a good chunk of the apartment. "I don't know. You might be able to find something decent for twenty thousand dollars."

He laughed. "Come on. I don't think she was that good."

"Actually," said Clara, "she was much better."

The husband stared at her—she thought it was disbelief at first, but then she realized his attention had veered to the window behind her. He excused himself and slipped out to the deck to join some men he referred to as "his boys." Clara waited for a minute before she decided to take a shot at insinuating herself into Jo's conversation zone. Jo didn't seem inviting; she kept smiling grimly then drifting off to wipe up invisible spills. Clara was only drinking club soda but she began to feel a little drunk on her own hurt feelings. Jo could at least *speak* to her. They'd been important to each other once—at least, Jo had been important to her. She had a terrible urge to tell Jo how much she'd learned from her.

"I play a little like you now." Clara tried to keep her voice light, though she'd edged Jo into a corner of her kitchen, up against the big gas range and the spotlighted counters. "Less showmanship, more reflection. I try to, anyway."

"You do? Why?"

"Well, I just always admired that about you. It impressed me."

Jo inhaled deeply, the way she used to before she played a phrase on the violin. All expression drained out of her face except for a knot of tension in her jaw. To her surprise, Clara remembered what this look signified: fury. "Do me a favor and don't use me as your crutch," Jo said softly. "I don't want to be part of your little classical music club. I don't want to be part of anything so thankless and stupid and dead."

Clara stepped back, startled. "Oh. But you used to love it."

"I never loved it. I was just good at it. You *assumed* I loved it because you did, and everything was all about you: Clara, the big genius." Jo leaned against the range and spread her arms at either side. Even without the mark on her neck, she still looked as if she'd just broken free from a marauding strangler. "I never loved it. Playing classical music is like living in a museum. It's lifeless, dead, dull. I don't even *like* it."

Clara touched her chest; she felt a fuzz of confusion scrambling her brain. "It's just that you were so good. I always wondered how you could give it up. I thought—" she paused, half-afraid that Jo was a little crazy. It wasn't all about her, was it? But Jo had always been too smart to make things up out of the blue. "I just thought it might be difficult. I just thought you might miss the music." Or, she thought, me.

"Well, maybe you think that, but I'm doing great. My days don't revolve around whether or not I've been a good girl and practiced until my neck bleeds. I don't have to do everything right all the time. I don't punish myself. I'm not a violinorexic."

"Violinorexic?" Clara couldn't help it, she laughed at the word. Then, to her surprise, Jo laughed too.

Clara's mother tapped her on the shoulder. She was holding her coat in her arms. Her mother turned to Jo. "Clara has to go now," she said. "Clara's playing with the Phil tonight! Jon Bon Jovi is conducting!"

"Mother," Clara slid her arms into the coat, "it's Joseph Bonaventura, and please don't lecture Jo."

Her mother ignored her and continued. "I can get you tickets, Jo. I know you would love it. You should read her reviews: the great cellist! Plays like a dream! Such sensitivity!"

Jo crossed her arms over her chest. "That's fabulous. Just fucking fabulous."

Clara looked at Jo and saw it: the pursed lips, the white knuckles, the ruddy flush. It was hate, plain and simple. Jo hated her. Her friend *hated* her. For a second she felt as if all the air had been sucked out of the room. Then, without a word, Clara turned and walked out of the apartment. She made her way to the elevator and rode it to the lobby, wiping at her tears with a tissue, trying to save her makeup. She couldn't understand it. It had always been a mystery to her. Jo had so much—so much talent, so much beauty—why had she always wanted what Clara had, too?

When she arrived backstage at Avery Fisher Hall, Clara changed, brushed her hair until it frizzed with static, tuned, warmed up, and tuned again. A moment before she walked onstage, she had an extraordinary spell of nerves. While she stood in the wings, peeking out at the audience, she felt completely undone by Jo's venom: maybe Jo was right. Maybe she was still a child. Maybe she really was fat and ugly and self-centered and talentless. But then she took a step forward and the world she knew cascaded back into place. *Everything's great.* She felt the familiar weight of her cello, the height of the hall opening around her, the tempo of the piece she was about to play thumping in her chest. She strode onstage and nodded to the conductor. They were performing the Dvořák cello concerto, one of her favorites. As always happened with a piece she knew so well, she sensed all of her teachers crowding into her mind, scolding and encouraging, and her parents, and old friends and lovers. But as she took her seat, it was still Jo's voice that she listened to the most attentively. It told her to slow down, to think, to be true to the music, to avoid the easy gesture. It told her to listen to her heart; of course, Jo had never said anything like that, but maybe she'd secretly wanted to. Maybe she'd secretly been overflowing with love all the time: beneath the hate, beneath the jealousy, even beneath the intelligence. Even if it wasn't exactly true, like so many things in life, there was no one to stop her from pretending that it was.

Then Clara bent her head, put her bow to the string, and began to do what she'd been practicing forever since she was a little girl: playing the most beautiful music in the world.

Acknowledgments

Grateful acknowledgment is made to the editors of the following publications, in which these stories first appeared: "Twin Study" in *Zoetrope All-Story*, 2004; "The Cavemen in the Hedges" in *Zoetrope All-Story*, 2000; "Christ, Their Lord" in *Tin House*, 2004; "Habits and Habitat of the Southwestern Bad Boy" in *Hayden's Ferry Review*, 2001; "Blackout" in *Spork*, 2004; "My Mother the Rock Star" in *Mississippi Review*, 2002; "Young People Today" in *Ontario Review*, 2004; "The Land of Pain" in *Willow Springs*, 2005; "A Case Study of Emergency Room Procedure and Risk Management by Hospital Staff Members in the Urban Facility" in *The Insomniac Reader: Stories of the Night*, 2005.